A HOME IN THE MIST V

A CADES COVE STORY

TENDER MERCIES
PART I

W.T. RIDENOUR

A HOME IN THE MIST V

A Cades Cove Story

TENDER MERCIES
PART I

W. T. Ridenour

Author photo © 2020 by Kathy Ridenour
Cover photo AI generated image by foupax (Pixabay)
Cover design © 2023 Timothy M. Ridenour

Edited and formatted by Timothy M. Ridenour

Published by WTR Books.

ISBN 978-1-7358587-7-7

In Loving Memory Of

Cheryl S. Justice

1954 – 2023

&

As Always

To Kathy

Table Of Contents

ONE

Awakening

A MALE VOICE FILTERED INTO the tranquility of my subconscious mind.

"Time to wake up, Billy."

It was a pleasant tone, and not in the least bit threatening, yet I resisted the call. I was in a warm, comfortable place and didn't wish to be bothered.

Please go away, I thought.

A cool, damp cloth soothed my forehead and cheeks. It felt good. I began to emerge from the dark.

"He's coming 'round," I heard someone say.

Hesitantly, I opened one eye. When it didn't explode, I opened the other.

"There you are," the voice said.

It was Doc Dulaney. Over his shoulder, I could see

a worried smile on Ma's face.

"Hate to bother your slumber," Doc said, "but it's about time for you to return to the living."

"Hello, ahem," I coughed weakly then sipped from the glass of water Doc offered me.

"Hello, Doc, Ma," I said. "How long have I been here?"

"Four days now," Doc said. "I hear you had a nice visit with Mary Wilson yesterday."

I vaguely remembered Mary's face floating in front of me like a dream. If not for the doctor's mention of it, I wouldn't have believed it was real.

Was that yesterday?

As he talked, the doctor checked over my wounds. I hoped he wouldn't touch my nose cause it hurt something fierce. He didn't.

"You were real lucky," he said. "That pistol ball grazed a timber as it passed through the wall of that crib and deflected through your right shoulder. Not a pretty wound to be sure, but a broken collarbone and torn muscle is a lot better than a hole in the heart."

I nodded, and wished I hadn't.

"Course, that ain't all," he continued. "Two

chunks of shattered wood got ya too. One piece was about twelve-by-four inches, and three inches thick. It slapped you flat sided on the back. Did a lot of bruising and may have cracked a rib or two, but it could have been a whole lot worse. Another piece about six-inches-long and half-an-inch square pierced three inches into your right side. I got it out and don't think it hit anything vital, so mainly we're gonna have to keep an eye out for infection."

Leaning in closer than I felt comfortable with, he examined my face.

"Got ya a broken nose, two black eyes, and a few loose teeth, but that's no concern. Couple o' weeks and you'll forget all about 'em."

He winked and said, "Easy for me to say, huh."

Nodding at Ma who was now sitting on the bed with a hand on my leg, he said, "From what I hear, you got the best nurse around. I think you'll pull through just fine."

The doc patted my arm and stood up to leave.

"By the way," he said, "thanks for the business. My family was about to starve before I started carin' for you. I was beginnin' to think this must be the healthiest town in Tennessee. Now, all the sudden, I've got more business than you can shake a stick at."

I gave a lopsided grin and shrugged. Bad idea. That hurt too.

Dulaney chuckled as he put on his hat and picked up his bag. Placing a hand on Ma's shoulder, he said, "I think he's gonna be fine. I'll find my own way out."

I was later to learn that Diver had come to see me every evening after closing the mill. He'd just sat there quietly by my bed as I laid sleeping. It wasn't until the day Doc Dulaney woke me that we finally got a chance to talk. Sittin' on a chair next to my bed with a smile on his lips but pain in his eyes, he laid a gentle hand on my head and asked how I was feeling.

"Middlin'," I said, "but it's sure nice to see you."

With that, I mostly conserved my energy while he filled me in on all I'd missed while I slept away my days.

". . . and you might be interested to know that Casey went and retrieved that wagon of apples you left sittin' in the orchard and delivered them to Delma's store," he said. "They put up a big ol' sign that read, 'Billy's Beauties . . . No girl included'. They sold out in two days."

That kinda tickled me some, but it hurt when I laughed.

Diver went on to tell me that the day after Doc Dulaney spread word that he figured I'd pull through, a group of men from the Cove formed a posse to confront Hiram Haggen. On their way to his place, they met Buck Wheeler headed for town. Buck told 'em that the night before last, Pearle had showed up at his place and asked if he and Eunice would take in Colton. She said Hiram figures it was Cole that ratted him out, and she's plumb scared for the boy to ever come home again. How he figured Cole had told anybody, seein's how he doesn't talk, was beyond her, but she'd brought his clothes anyway.

Eunice was thrilled and said she'd be proud to have the boy.

Colton seemed mighty happy too.

Pearle also claimed the entire clan was headed out. Said they'd be gone by morning.

The posse went ahead and checked the Haggen place anyway. Sure enough, just as Pearle had said, they were long gone. Only signs of life left on the place was a red tail hawk eyein' an old possum sittin' on a woodpile.

I gotta say, I wasn't in the least bit sorry to hear they'd lit a shuck. I figured there wasn't nothin' but peace and quiet for the Cove from here on out.

Boy, oh, boy, was I wrong. But before we get into all that, I'd like to mention an odd event that happened one evening shortly before Diver left my bedside. Not sure that he was even aware of it.

We'd sat and talked well into the night. Much later than usual. In fact, I was beginning to hope that he wouldn't pay too heavy a toll for it when he opened the mill the next morning. Yet for some reason, he seemed hesitant to leave.

Not that I wanted him to leave, mind you. Any time I got to spend with Diver was special to me. Especially since he and Charlotte had moved down to the Cove, and I didn't get to see him every day.

As it got late, my eyes became heavy and began to droop. I sank deeper into my pillow. In short order, I assume he thought I'd dosed off, but in truth, I was listening to his gentle voice and marveling at how it soothed my pain. He spoke of our time together and how much joy it had brought him . . . of how knowing me even for a short while had given his life meaning.

Then in a voice so soft I thought I must have misheard, he said, "As God is in heaven, one day we will meet again."

I half opened one eye and noticed a trail of moisture slowly trickle down his flushed cheek. I was a bit puzzled, as you might imagine, but just laid still and didn't draw attention to it.

As he sat there with a far-away look on his face, he reached down and squeezed my arm.

"Good night, Dennis," he whispered.

He then quietly rose and let himself out into the lonely night.

I'll admit, I wept for my friend that night. Time and again he had selflessly given of himself to benefit his neighbors, never asking for recompence. Never counting his end. Always leading by example as if to show us what life could be if only we bestowed God's tender mercies upon one another.

Yet, with all his compassion and understanding, he'd been unable to come to terms with the loss of his beloved son. His light.

It's true, he looked upon me as kind of a surrogate for Dennis, but I assure you, I was woefully unworthy of the honor.

Most in the Cove weren't even aware of Diver's inner turmoil as he wasn't one to wear his misery on his sleeve. They only saw benevolence and compassion. A man of peace—at peace.

Those of us who did know, could do nothing more than be there when his darker moments tried to overwhelm him.

Only Ma and Charlotte understood the depths of his sorrow. They had both been there themselves. We prayed the birth of his and Charlotte's miracle child would bring the comfort he so deserved.

A couple days after what Casey called, "my awakening," and Pa referred to as "my most elaborate scheme yet to get out of doing chores," Mary paid me another visit.

She was dressed just as pretty as you please in a newly sewn cornflower blue, plaid, print dress, interlaced with lime green and white highlights. On her head she wore a wide-brimmed, straw sun hat tied under her chin with a silky blue ribbon.

Looking at that dress, along with her crystal blue eyes and cascading blond hair, I reckoned there must be more than a few shame-faced angels out there quietly tiptoeing away to hide behind some nearby cloud for fear of being compared to her.

Ma had led her into my room before standing back with a lightly veiled smirk on her face as I struggled to close my yap. How my lower jaw had come to rest on my bare chest, I didn't know.

"Hey, Billy," Mary said, standing there with her hands clasped behind her back.

I immediately grabbed my sweaty cover with both hands and pulled it up tight under my chin. A faint groan escaped my lips as I thought about my damp, unwashed hair. What I wouldn't have given for ten minutes in that cold stream outside and a bar of Ma's best lye soap.

"Hey, Mary," I uttered.

Mary averted her eyes to the floor as she gently bit her lower lip. The flawless skin of her rosy cheeks radiated a soft pinkish glow that somehow warmed the back of my neck from all the way across the room. Then, all innocent like, but with what I'm sure was a well-practiced move, she once again floored me with that enchanting sideways peek she did so well from under the brim of her hat.

I reckon I must have visibly flinched when I bit my tongue 'cause Ma was struggling not to chuckle as she quickly turned and left the room.

How do you like that! My own mother had thrown up her hands in defeat and left me to face the bewildering world of feminine wiles all by my lonesome. You'd think I'd already proven just how woefully incompetent I was at that game by the fact that I was lying in bed looking like I'd gone nine rounds with Mr. Grear's prize bull.

"I've come to see how you're doin', Billy," Mary said. "And to show you the new dress I'm fixin' to wear to Cat Eye McGarity's Harvest Festival Hoedown in Tuckaleechee Cove."

"It's right pretty, Mary," I said.

"Oh, Billy, do ya mean it?" she gushed as she did a quick spin in the middle of the floor.

"Ain't never seen a blue-ribbon sow scrubbed in buttermilk that could shake a corn shuck at it," I boasted.

A subtle look of bewilderment crept across her face before she accepted that it must have been a compliment.

"Why, thank you, Billy," she said as she beamed with pride. "Now tell me that you'll be up and about in time to take me to the dance. It's not till the last weekend in September. You got nearly six weeks to heal."

I pretended I had to think about that for a moment.

"Oh please, Billy," she said as she stamped her foot. "We already missed Orwell Beckett's Independence Day dance, what with me travelin' and you gettin' kidnapped and all."

I looked at her pleading face and didn't have the heart to tease her further. Breakin' into a big smile, I said, "Of course, I'll take you to the hoedown, Mary. Even if I have to tie this bed behind Mac and Cornpone and drag it plumb to Tuckaleechee Cove. You can count on me. We're goin' dancin'."

"Whee!" cried Mary as she twirled around. "Now all I gotta do is convince Pa to let me go."

She rushed toward the door before stoppin' for

just a moment. Lookin' back, she said, "But, if it's all the same with you, I'd rather not drag the bed along."

She giggled and waved, then hurried out.

A few minutes later, Ma brought me my lunch. Noticing Mary was gone she said, "That was a short visit."

Grinnin', I said "Yeah, I think she hurried home to get ready for our dance."

"Dance!" Ma exclaimed. "In your condition?"

I started to laugh, then grabbed my side and oohed as a sharp pain wracked my cracked ribs. Lookin' into Ma's concerned face, I released a stifled breath and croaked, "It's not for six weeks, Ma. Hopefully, I'll be back among the living by then."

Ma sighed in relief. "With God's help," she said. Then steppin' closer, she placed my meal on my lap. "Now eat your lunch."

"Thanks, Ma," I said as she turned to leave. Then I said, "Oh, by the way."

She stopped and looked back.

"Reckon I might be able to take a bath today?"

Why, by the stunned look on her face, you'd have thought I asked her to sew a sun dress for my dog,

Baby. Course, I don't guess I can blame her. After all, it *was* the first time in fifteen years I'd actually *asked* to take a bath.

Ma thought about it for a bit, then said, "Well, the wash tub won't do. It's too small. In your condition, you couldn't get in there if you wanted to. And a sponge bath ain't gonna come close to gettin' that corn crib dust off o' ya."

She grimaced and shook her head as if contemplating an unpleasant thought. "If ya promise to be real careful with that shoulder and them ribs of yours, I'll see if Casey and your pa can get ya down to the stream tonight."

Then, looking at the crumpled bed, she said, "Give me a chance to change the linens too."

"About that," I said. "Ya think you could fix up the mat in the kitchen for me? I'd feel better bein' 'round folks 'stead of hid away back here by myself all day."

I could see in Ma's eyes she knew I was just tryin' to give her and Pa their bed back.

"You sure?" she said. "This bed's a lot more comfortable than that old sleepin' mat."

"I reckon if that mat was good enough for Diver

13

after comin' over them falls, and Casey after bein' snake bit, it'll do just fine for me after bein' roughed up by the Haggens," I said.

"Roughed up, is it now?" Ma said. She smiled and kissed me on the forehead.

"You're a good boy," she said. "I'll do it, but if you take to hurtin' too much, you let me know. Your pa and I can get along fine without our bed for a few weeks."

"If I take to hurtin', I'll let you know," I promised.

With that, Ma fixed up the sleepin' mat in the kitchen just as comfortable as you please, and I waited for Pa and Casey to get home.

It seemed like a long wait at the time, but I'll tell ya, if I knowed what I had comin', I could a done a heap more waitin'. When they got there and went to helpin' me hobble down to that brook, it weren't no fun at all. I reckon there was folks down in the Cove lookin' at the hills, wondering what all the strange caterwaulin' was all about.

But at least, when it was all said and done, I'm proud to say, I did get me a bath that night. Yes, sir, I muddied that stream somethin' fierce.

14

TWO

Hello Little One

WEEKS PASSED AS MY BODY HEALED. It was a bit touch and go there for a while, but with the resilience of youth, I was up and about sooner than Ma thought prudent. Course, I was under strict orders from Doc Dulaney to take it slow and easy and be sure not to lift anything that might hamper the healing of my bones.

"Ain't no splintin' a rib or collarbone," he said. "Ya just gotta let 'em get re-acquainted."

As I recall, I put on a fair show o' mopin' and frettin' about, and bein' plumb distressed over not bein' able to do my chores and carry my weight around the place.

"If only Dulaney would back off and let me help," I lamented, as I rocked on the porch drinking a cold glass of sassafras tea with baby curled up at my feet.

Not that my performance held a candle to Pa's, mind you.

Why, it was downright heartrendin' to see the toll all that extra work was takin' on his frail, over-stressed body.

Course, he'd not complain any.

No, sir, he seldom said a word about it at all. He'd just pat me on the shoulder as he hobbled through the kitchen tryin' valiantly to drag himself to the supper table. Nary a peep passed his lips other than an ooh here, or an aah there— and perhaps a pained moan as he tried to sooth a back spasm while feebly lowering himself onto his favorite kitchen chair.

Like to make ya swell up and burst with pride just bein' in the presence of a man who could accomplish such a Herculean task. And him being so late in his hard-earned golden years. All with no regard for his own welfare either. None at all.

"Just doing what's gotta be done for the good of the family," he'd say.

'Bout brought a tear to my eyes; I don't mind tellin' ya.

16

'Course, Ma wasn't 'bout to tip the fiddler for either one of us. Said she'd heard better tub-thumpin' from that peddler fella that once tried to sell her a contraption he claimed would wash her laundry while she cranked a handle.

"Who's ever heard of such a thing?" I remember her scoffin'. "As if a body needs a machine to do their washin'. That thing ain't never gonna sell."

While me and Pa both strove to maintain a stiff upper lip and not burden others with our plight in life, Charlotte was at the B&C Emporium looking over a bolt of green floral calico.

She'd just examined a couple yards of the fabric to see how many blemishes and imperfections it had and was in the process of refolding it when she felt a spasm of her own. A quick, sharp, clinching sensation; not unlike what you might feel when gulping a glass of ice-cold spring water on a really hot summer's day.

It wasn't an overwhelming pain, but it did catch her attention. After all, her time *was* near.

Pausing, she laid the material on the counter and placed a hand on her tight stomach.

Was that a one-time twitch or are things about to

17

get underway? she pondered.

Time passed. A small bell tingled as a customer left the store. A bluebottle fly made a nuisance of himself buzzing around her head.

Suddenly a much sharper pain racked her body.

Grabbin' the counter with both hands, she bent over and groaned. The bolt of fabric shifted sending a pair of long bladed cuttin' scissors clatterin' to the floor.

Delma glanced back from where she was clinging to a ladder restockin' a shelf with The Cades Cove Methodist Ladies' Benevolence Society's assortment of hand-woven baskets, alongside Hec Rucker's hammered copper cookware. She saw Charlotte scrunched over with jaws clinched tight in pain.

"Oh, my word," she murmured, scrambling off the ladder, and hurryin' to Charlotte's aid.

Charlotte was starin' at the floor, watching as the rough-cut planking slowly darken around the hem of her long dress.

"I think it's time," she hissed as another jolt nearly buckled her knees. "Ooowww," she groaned. Then looking at Delma, she said, "Sorry about your

18

floor."

Delma swept a stack of folded towels and wash cloths off a low standing rack and helped Charlotte sit down.

"Don't be silly," she said. "You ain't got a thing to be sorry about."

Then straightenin' up and glancin' around, she said, "Wait right here. I'll be back."

Rushing to the door, she flung it open and was surprised to see James' sorrel and Pat Tudwell's bay both tied to the hitchin' post out front. The two men were sittin' on the wide porch deep in concentration over a highly contested game of checkers. It wasn't uncommon for James to be occupied in such pursuits on workin' days when Delma could use his help in the store.

"James!" Delma gasped. "Charlotte's time is come! Hurry over and get Diver. Tell him to bring his buggy. Then go get Doc Dulaney."

"Doc's out at Hickory Flats," James said. "Robby Lindsey come down sick after steppin' on one of them little stingin' catfish. Must o' got him real good, I reckon. I doubt the doc'll be back before nightfall at the soonest."

"Well then, go get Mable Davis. Sarah May too, while you're at it."

Looking at Pat she said, "And you go fetch my ma. She'd skin the bunch of us alive if we left her outta this. Now get to it, the both of ya."

As Delma rushed back in to be at Charlotte's side, Pat looked at James. "Reckon we got our marchin' orders," he quipped with a smile on his face.

"Yeah, reckon so," said James, a bit red faced.

He didn't like Pat thinkin' Delma wore the pants in the family.

"I always say," he continued, "when it comes to them female situations, you just gotta step back and let the women do what women do best."

"Right," said Pat as he stuffed his hat on his head and stood up. "When it comes to them female situations. I'll see ya later."

Leavin' the game half played, he hurried to his horse and with a "yip" soon had the pretty bay whipped into a full gallop headed for the Banion homestead.

James, feeling a bit put-out, slapped his own hat

upside his leg and tried not to grind his teeth as he contemplated Pat's retort. Kinda sounded like Tudwell wasn't buying that he ruled his own roost. That was a misconception that was gonna have to be eradicated. Climbin' on his horse, he yanked his sorrel's head about and gigged it toward Diver's mill.

≈

In barely an hour, Charlotte was clinchin' the covers in her own bed while Mable, Ma, Sarah May, and Delma, did all they could to make her comfortable. From the way the labor pains were advancing, Mable said it wouldn't be long now.

Ma and Sarah May agreed.

Mable wiped Charlotte's sweat beaded brow with a cool cloth and told her she was doin' real good.

"This uns fixin' to meet the folks."

Charlotte nodded and tried to smile but was wracked with the hardest contraction yet.

"That's fine," said Mable lettin' Charlotte squeeze her arm though she knew she'd have a whopper of a bruise come mornin'.

"It's almost over."

While the women fretted over Charlotte, Pa and Forrest helped Diver tromp a trail into his front porch planking. They tried to keep his mind occupied by debatin' the likelihood of bein' snowbound come winter versus hampered with a bone-chillin' freeze and not enough precipitation.

"I'd just as well have the snow myself," said Pa. "Them deep freezes is hard on the land."

"Hard," said Diver.

Pa wasn't sure if Diver was following the conversation or speakin' of Charlotte.

As everyone else was either gathered 'round Diver or Charlotte awaiting on the big event, I was stuck at home by myself. I had no idea what was goin' on.

So much for havin' a sleepin' mat in the kitchen where I could join in the conversation.

"Waahhh!"
Diver's knees like to've buckled, but Pa and Forrest each grabbed an arm and held him up.

"Hang in there, old man," Pa said. "I reckon ya got yourself a young'un."

Diver still looked a bit unsteady on his feet but had a smile on his face that downright tickled both Pa and Forrest.

Father and son shook hands and slapped each other on the back lookin' to all the world like it was they who had accomplished something.

A few minutes later the front door opened, and Ma said to Diver, "Would you like to come see your new daughter?"

"Daughter?" Diver burst. He grabbed Pa's shoulders, then pulled him in for a big hug. "I got me a daughter!"

Pa spun Diver around and said, "Well, let's go make her acquaintance."

As they entered the crowded bedroom, Diver hurried to Charlotte's side.

"I got a daughter," he told her. "I mean we've got a daughter," he corrected.

Charlotte laughed.

"Yes, we have a daughter," she said. "And she's a beauty."

Then reaching out the small bundle, she asked, "Would you like to hold her, Papa?"

Diver looked a bit shell shocked. It was as if he didn't know what to do. He looked at Ma.

Ma smiled and nodded. "Take her," she said. Her eyes were brimming in tears.

Wipin' both hands on his shirtfront, Diver hesitantly took the bundle. He gently cradled it in his arms, looked at all the smilin' faces around him, then slowly pulled back the edge of the blanket. Inside was the most startling sky-blue eyes he'd ever seen. Father and daughter looked into each other's faces as if they were the only two people in the room.

"Hello little one," Diver said. "Hello...?"

He looked at Charlotte. "What's her name?" he asked.

"I thought we'd call her Pauline," Charlotte said. "After your mother."

Diver's chest swelled with gratitude. He couldn't think of a better tribute to honor the mother he'd lost at such an early age.

"She'd be so proud," he said.

Lookin' back at the baby he said, "Hello, Pauline."

"Pauline Kathryn," Charlotte said, smilin' at Ma. "Pauline Kathryn McCoy."

Ma's eyes widened as she clasped her hands to her breast. "Me?" she said.

Charlotte laughed as she held her hand out to Ma. Tears of joy rolled down her face.

"I'll never forget what you did for my Diver," she said, taking Ma's fingers and squeezing them. "Zeb may have pulled him from that pool, but you nursed him back to health and took him in when he was in need. If not for you and your family, I may have lost him forever."

Ma nearly squealed as she rushed over and gave Pa a big hug. Pa just stood there beaming, one hand cradled around Ma's back and the other squeezin' Diver's shoulder.

Yeah, I reckon it was a grand ol' time in that little bedroom in the Cove. I'm mighty sorry I missed it.

≈

You know, I've heard it said; "When the way is clear, and ya got the wind to your back, you may as well have a good run. The trail ahead will slow ya down soon enough."

And so, it was with me. I was feelin' good. It had been a week since Pauline was born and Ma finally let me ride to the Cove with Pa so I could meet her. She was about the sweetest little thing I'd ever seen. Truth be told, I think she took to me some too.

While we were there, I ambled out to the mill to watch Diver ply his trade. It never ceased to amaze me how he could judge the grit of any ground grain by no more than rubbing it between his thumb and index finger. Even in a darkened mill! And he knew what every farmer preferred from his harvest too.

On top of all that, he told me, you gotta keep close attention to the smell of the stones. It wouldn't do to burn the grain.

He said, "In fact, eighty percent of the grinding process is done by smell. A miller's gotta always keep his nose to the grindstone. Too much or too little air in the furrows; not enough grain in the hopper; maybe even a misalignment of stones; it can all cause scorched or burnt flour at the least, and an explosion at the worst. People don't realize it, but wheat, oat, barley, and rye dust is more explosive than high-grade gunpowder. Coal dust is downright safe compared to it. Only corn and buckwheat is less volatile, though it should still be handled with caution."

As I watched Diver work, my attention was distracted by the clatterin' sound of wagon wheels out front. Goin' to the door, I looked out.

There, in the shade of a big oak tree, sat the Widow Rollins in what may have been the most dilapidated buckboard that ever stirred up a dust trail in southern Appalachia. The old sway-backed draft horse she had in harness should have been turned out to pasture about a decade before her late husband, Effy, passed from the ague five years back.

The widow sat there, thumpin' her cane on the floorboard, waitin' for somebody to come by and give her a hand.

Hurryin' down the millhouse steps the best I could, tryin' not to re-injure my wounds, I offered to help the widow from her wagon.

"I ain't that old, young man," she said as she climbed down on her own. "But you can grab my poke o' nubbins."

I looked into the bed of the buckboard and saw a small gunny sack of corn kernels that couldn't have amounted to much more than twenty pounds or so. Glancing around to make sure Pa wasn't watchin', I reached in with my good arm and lifted out the bag.

It wasn't of no account, but I'm sure Ma would o' preferred I'd left it for someone else to tote.

"You're Zeb Banion's boy, ain't ya?" the widow asked.

"I surely am," I said.

"Humph," was all the reply she made before turnin' and climbin' the mill steps.

What that meant, I don't know. I just followed with her sack of grain.

"Hello, Mrs. Rollins," Diver said as he came over to the doorway and took both her hands. "How are you doin' this fine day?"

"Well, I'm ailin' a bit preacher," she said. "What, with a crick in my neck every time I lay down and try to sleep, and the lumbagos actin' up in my back when it rains."

She rubbed her lower back as if to validate the problem.

"Not to mention a whole passel of corns on the bottom of my feet. Why, I feel like I'm walkin' barefoot in a field of sweetgum balls every time I take a step."

She dabbed a linen kerchief on her cheeks and mouth before replacin' it in a pocket.

"Course, you know, I'd never be one to mention it."

"Of course not," said Diver.

Taking the bag from me, he said, "So, what do we have here?"

Running his thumb over a handful of wrinkled kernels, he let 'em slip back through his fingers. They was some mighty poor specimens if ya asked me.

"That's all the corn I got, Preacher," said the widow. "I know it ain't worth your time, but I's hopin' you could grind 'em for me."

"Why, sure," said Diver placin' the bag on a scale.

From where I stood, I could see it was twenty-four pounds.

"As I recall, you like extra fine cornmill," he said.

"If it ain't too much trouble," the widow said, payin' close attention to the brass pointer on Driver's scale.

Diver scooped ten pounds of healthy corn from a bushel basket and poured it into the hopper.

"It'll take just a moment for me to adjust the stones," he said.

The widow nodded as he delicately tapped the screw handle lowering the top stone ever so slightly to the bedstone.

After he was satisfied with the grit, he added Mrs. Rollins' nubbins and milled the whole lot.

"There ya be," he said as he lifted her sack of freshly ground cornmill from the flour chest.

It was noticeably heavier than the one she'd brought in.

"I already cut out my ten percent miller's fee, so the rest is all yours."

He handed the bag to me to return to her buckboard. A few small shakes told me it was indeed heavier.

"Sounds a bit steep to me," the widow said. "But I reckon it's only half o' what that crook at Bender's Mill charged me."

"Now, I'm sure Mr. Bender's a right fine miller,"

Diver said.

"Humph," said Mrs. Rollins as she ushered me out the door.

Then, just as she was leavin', she said, "Thanks preacher."

"You're very welcome," said Diver.

As Mrs. Rollins rode away, I stood near the hitchin' post and looked up at the darkened entryway of the mill. Scratchin' my ear, I contemplated for a moment. As I recollected, Diver ground ten pounds of good grain as he adjusted the stones before addin' Mrs. Rollins' twenty-four pounds of nubbins. That's an extra thirty percent added to the mix. He then took ten percent of the total as the miller's fee.

Seemed like mighty poor math for a businessman.

But then again, it seemed just about right for Diver.

THREE

Dance Partner

WELL NOW, THAT'S WHAT I was talkin' about. As my body healed, it seemed as if I had the wind at my back and I was feelin' good. The way ahead was clear with no obstacles in site. I was runnin' down the trail of life with abandon—kickin' up my heels like a young colt, sure that nothin' could stop me now.

Then, just as the proverb said it would, the way ahead put a big ol' toe-stubbin' rock smack dab in the middle of my path. Slowed me down, right quick, it did.

Truth be told; it dumped me flat on my face.

From euphoria to despair, and me not knowin' how I got there.

If you're wonderin' just what that rock was? Why, it was my own sweet Mary Wilson!

Yeah, you heard right. It was little Mary Wilson who knocked the wind plumb outta my sails.

It started out as a mighty fine day. One of those serene, feel-good days when a cool breeze wafts down off the higher peaks breaking up the long, hot, dog days of autumn. A day when dirty-faced boys are apt to be seen draped over large, sturdy limbs in their favorite climbin' tree, while young, giggling girls congregate in the yard of the mom with the best sweet milk and cookies. More often than not they'd be lookin' quite prudish in their fancy bows and lace, while teachin' their favorite homemade dolls what Miss Shelley says every young woman ought to know.

I'd recently been okayed by Doc Dulaney—but more importantly by Ma, to recommence doing some of my lighter chores like milkin' and feedin' stock. Not that that was a good thing in itself, but it opened the way for me to engage in many of my more enjoyable pursuits.

Upon finishin' my mornin' chores, I had Baby all in a tither, hoppin' around, wantin' to know where we were headed as I gathered up my best fishin' pole and a handful of homemade hooks.

I'd discovered that the little pool at the entrance of Casey's canyon was a mighty fine place for catchin' brook trout and I figured on surprisin' Ma with a whole batch of 'em for supper.

Problem is, I dawdled around just a bit too long gettin' ready.

As I strolled along the pathway that leads through the brambles to the canyon, I was hummin' a little ditty to myself that Casey said he'd heard in a showhouse up in Illinois. It was something I don't reckon Ma would have been all that pleased with, but I saw no harm in it.

I hadn't gone far at all when I heard the familiar sound of a tinklin' bell driftin' through the trees behind me.

Mary?

Yes. I knew that sound. That was the jangle of the little golden bell Pastor Wilson had attached to Fancy's halter when he decided he couldn't stop Mary from ridin' up the Cove Trail to visit with me and Ma.

He said it would give wild creatures a warnin' that

she was comin' so they wouldn't accidentally stumble into each other.

I suppose he was right, but I figured in all likelihood, Pa had cleared our neck of the woods of dangerous critters many years ago.

Course, I reckon there ain't no accountin' for a stray panther now and again. A fact me and Henry can attest to.

Having heard the bell, I turned back.

I can tell ya, Baby wasn't none too happy about that at all. She proceeded to pouncin' around, pawin' at my legs, and gettin' under foot until I finally had to push her away and snap, "What's got into you!"

At that, she finally backed off and dolefully followed behind, head and tail both hangin' low.

I reckon there's a heap o' fellas out there that would o' done well to listen to their dogs. And I was soon to learn, I was one of 'em.

"Yo, Mary!" I called as I exited the woods. "Mary, over here."

Since she'd been concentratin' on the house and barn, my sudden shout from behind nearly caused her to fall off Fancy as they spun around.

There I stood with a goofy, apologetic grin on my face, a fishin' pole clutched in my raised right hand, and Baby slinkin' around, occasionally pressing her head against my leg. It later occurred to me that she may have been questioning just how utterly stupid her human could be.

"There you are!" Mary shouted. "And don't you dare, 'Yo, Mary!' me."

What? What did that mean?

"I'm so mad I could take a horse whip to ya without a blush at next Sunday's prayer meetin'."

I reckon that you might figure after facin' a killer panther, bein' lost in an unescapable cave, and havin' Clayton Haggen hold a loaded pistol to my back; I just couldn't be intimidated no more. Well, you'd be wrong. I didn't even know what I'd done, but I panicked.

"I can explain," I blurted.

As Mary gigged Fancy across the yard toward me, she said, "What can you explain?"

"Huh," I said.

Mary reined back on Fancy and glared at me.

My mind was in a whirl. I didn't know what I'd

done, when I'd done it, or why I was even apologizing. All I wanted was to go fishin'.

I looked at Baby for an answer.

Lookin' me in the face, she sneezed, then turned and walked into the underbrush.

Thanks a lot, I thought. Now I was truly alone.

"Okay," I said to Mary. "I *can't* explain. But that's because, whatever it is, I didn't do it."

Mary's eyes lit up like a lightning struck tree on a moonless summer's night. If you ain't never seen such a thing, I can tell ya, it's a frightful sight.

"Are you saying you didn't dance with Ally Haggen?!" she spat.

What? Ally Haggen? What brought that up?

"Don't you lie to me, Billy Banion," Mary growled as her piercing blue eyes pinned me to the spot I was standin' on. "Francis Beaman, Dotty Pike, and Susan Beckett, all saw you dancin' with Ally Haggen at Hec and Charlie's wedding. They said you were the talk of the town."

"Oh, is that all," I said.

I've never said four words I so wanted to take back in all my life.

37

"Oh, is that all?" screamed Mary. "IS THAT ALL!"

"I didn't mean it like that," I groaned.

Somehow the day had suddenly gotten awfully hot. My ears felt like they were on fire, sweat was runnin' down my cheeks, and I could feel my heart poundin' like a barn swallow with a tomcat standin' on his tail.

"I mean, it didn't *mean* anything," I said.

"Then why didn't you tell me about it?" she pleaded.

I could see the hurt in her eyes.

"Because, I didn't think about it," I tried to explain. "It was meaningless. A fluke." Then true inspiration struck me. "In fact, it was nothing more than an accident."

"An ACCIDENT?" She exploded. "You were dancing with Ally Haggen, the girl you would latter get caught kissing in *our* orchard, because she fell into your arms by accident?"

"Yes," I said trying hard to show the sincerity on my face.

"OH, BILLY," shrieked Mary. She now had tears runnin' down her face. "You expect me to believe you *accidentally* danced with that girl?"

"Yes," I said. "I mean, no. It was an accident when she fell into my arms, not when we . . ."

I could hear a high-pitched squeal startin' to emanate from Mary's throat. Truth be told, it was a bit discombobulating.

"What I mean is." My thoughts were so scrambled by that point, I didn't really know what was gonna come out of my mouth next. "Well, you see, we were watchin' the dance together."

The squeal picked up an octave.

I stopped to refocus.

"I don't mean we were together," I said. "I mean, I was standin' there, and she was standin' next to me."

That didn't really help. Mary's face was reddening, and I could see poor Fancy's nostrils swell as she tried to take in the breath that Mary was squeezin' out of her.

"Anyway," I rambled on, rather than just shuttin' my big mouth, "all of the sudden, she tripped and grabbed for me on the way down. As you can imagine, there wasn't a thing I could do but grab her back," I explained. "Just to keep her from fallin', and all. What

39

else *could* I do?"

I spread my arms to indicate the innocence in the whole affair.

"And that's how it happened," I said. "It was nothin' but an accident."

"She tripped while just standin' there with you and you both wound up dancin' so she wouldn't fall?" snapped Mary. "That's what your tellin' me?"

"No, you got it all wrong, Mary," I pleaded. "Why, the dance didn't even come until later. You see, Ally was holding my arm and . . ."

The shriek finally came out.

Fancy jumped as if snake bit. She crow-hopped with wide eyes and raised ears, tryin' to figure out where the shrill noise was comin' from. Wherever it was, she didn't like it one bit. In an instant, she was flying across the yard at top speed.

Jostled and bounced, Mary reeled from one side of the saddle to the other. Her bonnet pulled loose and flapped about, tangled in her wildly flailing hair. I could plainly hear the painful clack of teeth along with a sputtering, oh! oh! oh! every time her backside made contact with the finely tooled leather.

I stood transfixed, not knowin' what to do.

Finally, after several harrowing seconds of unintended but quite impressive horsemanship, she found her seat and reined Fancy toward the Cove Trail. As she rode away, tears streamed from her eyes.

"Mary!" I cried, runnin' across the yard.

She didn't stop or even look back.

I stood there; crestfallen. Fishin' pole in hand. It had started as such a good day. Fact is, if you'd asked right then what had happened, I don't figure I could have even told ya.

It was then that Baby came slinkin' back out o' the brush.

"Coward," I said.

That evenin', I kept Ma company in her back kitchen as she made a smoked buffalo roast with a raspberry sauce glaze and boiled garden veggies.

No trout on the menu that night.

As she cooked, I tried to explain what had transpired between Mary and me down by the canyon trail.

"You mean you didn't tell her about dancin' with that Haggen girl?" she asked.

41

Ma still wasn't ready to call a Haggen by their first name. It was, "that Haggen girl," or "that Haggen boy," or "Old Man Haggen," or even "Buck's sister." Only Colton was referred to by his given name, but she considered him a Wheeler.

"No. It didn't occur to me," I said. "It was just a dance. It's not like we had a date or nothin'."

"Son," Ma said as she pursed her lips and shook her head, "you got a lot to learn about women."

I just sat there, lookin' down at my hands as I tried to smooth a chipped fingernail with a small knife I'd took to carryin'.

"I reckon so," I said. "Figure I should talk to Pa about it?"

Ma's hand shot to her mouth to cover a choked off snicker. Eyes wide, she turned her back to me as she tried unsuccessfully to regain control. Her shoulders rose and fell as she struggled to even her breathing. I heard some gargled cackles break loose followed by a sudden loud snort. A sound not unlike that made by the big boar hog me and Pa were fixin' to butcher in a few weeks.

That just got her even more tickled, is what it

done.

Turnin' back to me with tears streamin' down her face, she laid her hands on my shoulders.

"I'm sorry, honey," she gasped. "I love your pa, dearly. But understandin' women just ain't one of his strong suits."

She pressed her hands to her stomach and drew in two deep breaths.

"I reckon if I was you, I'd try Diver, or maybe Forrest."

She exhaled, seeming to finally get her breathin' under control.

"But certainly not your father," she giggled.

"Thanks, Ma," I said.

Standin', I pushed the chair back against the wall and went out to see what trouble Baby had gotten herself into. Before roundin' the corner of the house, I heard another peal of laughter.

Come Sunday, I couldn't wait to get to church and

see Mary.

I'd thought about Ma's advice to speak with Diver or Forrest, but under closer consideration I realized, there are some things a man just doesn't talk to other men about. I think it must be some kind of code men are just naturally born with.

Besides that, I'd come to realize, I didn't need help. I had this thing licked.

The Harvest Festival Hoedown was comin' up in less than two weeks. Mary would have to forgive me. There's no way she'd hold a grudge at me dancin' with Ally Haggen if it meant she'd miss out on the hoedown. Yeah, I was mighty proud of myself. This woman reasonin' thing wasn't no big deal after all.

As we pulled into the churchyard, I noticed a very handsome, midnight black, high gloss buggy with a set of brass carriage lamps pinned to each side. It had a single, coiled spring bench and a finely worked elk leather top that was dyed black and stitched with red thread.

To tell ya the truth, I don't figure I'd ever seen such a fine contraption. Not even those owned by Orwell and Mr. Grear.

The buggy was sittin' in the shade of a sugar maple tree and was harnessed to the reddest blood bay mare I ever seen.

"Who's that," I asked Pa as he set the brake.

"Don't know," he said. "Ain't never seen it before."

We climbed down, and after helpin' Ma get to her feet, went over to inspect the rig.

"Fine lookin' animal," said Pa as he scratched the horse's jaw and looked into its steady, clear eyes.

"Yep," I agreed. "She's a looker."

That was Pa for ya. Didn't even blink at the buggy. Went straight to the critter.

"Hello, Billy," I heard Mary say from behind us.

Me and Pa both turned around.

"Mary," Pa said as he tipped his hat before goin' over to join Ma where she stood greetin' Forrest and Sarah May.

"I see you're admirin' my ride to the dance," Mary continued.

"Your what?" I blurted. A lump was fast developing in my throat, and I was havin' a hard time talkin'. "I thought we'd take Pa's wagon."

"Yeah, I suspected you would," she said. "Course,

45

I hear your dance partner left town. However will you find her?"

This wasn't playin' out at all like I'd imagined it would.

"What are you talkin' about, Mary," I said.

"Hey there, Billy Goat Gruff," I heard.

With a groan, I turned around. *Tyrone? What was he doin' here? He's a Methodist.*

"So, what do you think about Pa's new buggy," he smirked. "I reckon Mary's gonna be a lot more comfortable in this then she would have been in your pa's old farm wagon. Way I hear it, it smells of mule droppings and rotten apples."

I looked at Mary.

"Tyrone?" I gasped.

"You've got your dance partner," she said, "I've got mine. 'Sides, Father said I couldn't go without a chaperone. I considered Second Chance, but his ma's still sick. So, Susan said she'd ride with us."

"But, why's he here?" I sputtered, pointin' at Tyrone. "He's a Methodist."

Tyrone was standin' back with his arms crossed and a grin on his face. He was enjoyin' the show.

46

"Father said if he was taking me, he'd first have to come by and get acquainted," she said as she took Tyrone's arm. "We figured what better time than Sunday mornin'."

"But, but."

I don't reckon my reply was quite snappy enough cause Mary said, "Come along, Tyrone."

Arm in arm, they headed for the church.

Just before they were lost in the dark interior, Mary looked back. I thought I saw sorrow in her eyes, but she quickly turned away and was gone.

I felt like I had a ten-pound catfish floppin' in my guts. Had all his fins extended too.

Losin' your gal is a mighty hurtful thing. Losin' her to Tyrone Beckett is about more then a body can stand.

FOUR

The Commitment

I'LL TELL YA, I WAS FEELIN' mighty low for a spell there. Just ain't nothin' that'll make a fella want to crawl under a fieldstone somewhere as seein' his gal with another beau. And of all people– TYRONE!

Why, the way I was mopin' around that place, it wasn't long before Baby started taggin' along with her head drooped so low her ears and tail was draggin' in the dust. If'n you'd have seen us I reckon you'd o' thought we were a mighty pitiful pair. Fact is, you'd o' been right.

Now, you may think I'm readin' too much into this whole thing. Perhaps I am? But it sure seemed to me like Ma's ol' rooster had a bit too much jubilation in his chortle every time I happened to pass his way. He'd go to prancin' back and forth, lookin' down on me, and cacklin' like an old hen.

Kinda grated on my nerves is what it done.

I got to thinkin' he was enjoyin' the show a bit too much. Course, lookin' back, I gotta admit, I *had* chuckled quite a bit when the women folk humiliated him the way they'd done. Perhaps a little tit for tat was justified. After all, call it a polecat or call it a skunk, ya ain't gonna mask the odor none either way. I was just pinin' too much to see it that way at the time.

Like I said, I was feelin' mighty low.

Course, lookin' back, it seems kinda odd in the tellin' of it that I didn't get comfortin' from my family. It wasn't that they didn't care. No, sir, that ain't it at all. They did care. How could ya not when you had someone like Diver showin' ya the way. It's just that sometimes life kinda takes ya where it wants to. It's not always easy to see someone else's burden when you're toting a load of your own.

Take Casey for example. Since he'd come home, me and him had not only become the brothers we were born to be, but true friends to boot. He had my back, and I knowed it. Thing is, as of late he'd become so enamored with his own sweetheart, he stumbled around like a man with blinders on.

Makes it hard to see someone else's plight when you're in a fog of your own.

As for Pa, I don't rightly know if he even noticed my melancholy. He never did quite know what to think about me and some of my antics.

When I did somethin' he approved of, just a nod of his head would make me swell up and be mighty proud. Though it's true, he never was one to cheapen praise by throwing it around like chicken feed to be strutted over and pecked at.

But when I did something knuckleheaded, well that seemed to confuse him somethin' fierce. He'd as likely as not push his hat back, scratch his noggin, shake his head, and just go on his way. Probably wonderin' if the defect was on his side or Ma's is what I'm thinkin'.

I remember one time when I nearly choked to death from accidentally swallowin' a tadpole while swimmin' down in Abrams Creek. I'll never forget the strange look in his eye when he found out about it. How he stared in Ma's face as if awaitin' the answer to an unasked question. He eventually simply shrugged his shoulders and shook his head as he said, "There's something wrong with that boy."

I'm embarrassed to admit, Ma couldn't come up with a reply.

Swallowin' a tadpole didn't make a lot of sense in Pa's world, so he just let it drop and walked away. Same thing applied with my morose mood over Mary, I suppose. He didn't comprehend the causation, so rather than interfere with what he didn't understand, he simply let it lie.

Ma, of course, knew exactly what my problem was. Though she didn't know the part about Tyrone and Mary fixin' to go to the dance together.

She'd given me what advice she could and figured I'd use it as I saw fit. I reckon it pained her heart somethin' fierce, but she was determined to let me stand on my own two feet. Let me be a man. She'd be there if she was needed.

I've known folks that never did understand that. They tried so hard to protect their children that in reality, they never gave 'em a chance to grow up. Caused more harm than good if you ask me. In the end, it plumb drove them away, is what it done.

I feel blessed for every stubbed toe and thorn prick I suffered along the way. Can't say I enjoyed it at the time, but it toughened me up enough to face the journey to come.

Anyway, I was feelin' some low, but didn't want to talk to no menfolk about it. It's true, Baby was a good listener, but she was mighty shy on advice. I was gettin' plumb disheartened. Then it struck me. Delma!

Delma had been away so long I'd gotten outta the habit of goin' to her. She always had the answer.

What I didn't know at the time was, Delma was one step ahead of me without even knowin' I was lookin' to lay my problems at her feet.

It seems, Mary and Charlotte happened to be at the B&C looking over a small blanket of brushed cotton that would be perfect for the new baby crib Charley Rucker had made for Pauline. Brushed cotton was certainly pricier than calico or linen, but warm and soft, and Charlotte felt it worth the cost for her darlin' baby.

As they discussed the merits of the fine material, an unexpected discourse began drifting through an open window from the side-yard below. It's not that they intended to hear the conversation, but rather that they could not avoid it.

"James, I need your help," Delma said loud enough to be clearly heard.

"Now, Delma," James replied with a bit of exasperation quite evident in his voice, "you know I'm a busy man."

There was a pause, then he continued.

"I can't drop everything every time you want to rearrange a display case or have a sparrow chased out of the rafters."

"Achoo!" Dolores Kilpatrick sneezed as she shook her head at Charlotte. "Plumb shame is what it is," she whispered, noddin' toward the window." Then seeing the material in Charlotte's hand, she reached out to feel it. "What a beautiful blanket. Sure, wish Ma could o' lived to see your little'un. Achoo! These dusty roads is 'bout to put me under too."

She suddenly went into a coughing fit.

"Oh dear! Oh dear!" She wiped her mouth and

waved as she headed toward the door. "I just can't wait no longer. Tell Delma I'll be back when she has more time."

There was another pause.

"Now, look here," James' voice carried through the window with a bit of desperation startin' to eke into it. "I'm the man of this house!"

"Yes, dear," Delma said, her voice soft and controlled.

Another dead pause. Charlotte looked at Mary and raised an eyebrow.

"Well, I am," James stated with a more hesitant timbre. "And what I say, goes."

"As it should," stated Delma.

"Huh?" from James.

"You are the man," said Delma. "A hard-workin' man. A loving husband and a protective father."

"Ah?" uttered James.

"A man that knows what's best for his family and sees to it that they are taken care of no matter the cost. No matter the burden placed on your own shoulders."

"Well, I try," James stammered.

"Yes, you do," said Delma. "And don't you let anyone say different."

James cleared his throat then and said, "You know, sometimes I can hardly sleep at night worryin' over you and little Jimmy."

"And I know it's the truth," claimed Delma. "Many a night I've lain there, weary to the bone after a long, hard day, and listened to you toss and turn trying in vain to get to sleep. Makes me wonder what kind of daily struggles a man must endure to leave him restlessly bereaved of sleep at the end of the day."

No reply from James.

"That's why it shames me so, when I have to ask you to give even more of yourself just because I'm a weak woman and incapable of doing what is mine to do. If only I were a better wife, you'd . . ."

"Oh, shush now," said James. "You're a wonderful wife. And you know you can ask anything of me. Anything at all."

"No, I don't want to burden you with my needs," Delma said. "I'll find some way to manage."

"Now, quit it," said James. "I can take a few minutes to help my sweetheart."

"You're sure?" asked Delma. "I don't want to keep you from what's really important. And whatever would the neighbors think if they saw you helpin' out with JJ and the store?"

"There's nothin' more important than you and JJ," said James. "Now you quit your frettin' and show me what you need done."

again,otte winked at Mary and covered her mouth as the voices faded for a moment before pickin' up again in the front doorway.

"Well, I've been hearin' from the ladies that Hec's cookware is too heavy for them to take down from the shelves," Delma said. "I thought if we hung it on the wall, it would be easier to manage."

As they walked toward the rack, she took James' arm in her hands and gently squeezed it.

"I could probably do it myself, but I figured as strong as you are . . ."

"Now, now," said James. "Say no more. I'll take care of it."

His chest swelled a bit as he flexed his bicep.

Delma stretched up and kissed him on the cheek. "Oh, thank you so much. You don't know what this means to me."

James smiled. "Not a problem, my dear," he said. "Not at all. You should know I'd never deny you anything."

Delma smiled back. "I'm so pleased."

As she turned to leave, she stopped and looked back. "Oh, one more thing. While I'm sorting through that new shipment of clothes, do you think you could sweep the floor. I'd be ever so grateful. It's getting a bit crusty in here. And while you're at it, them display cases on the north wall are gettin' pretty jumbled. They could use some rearrangin'. Then, if you'd be so kind, we need some more cheese brought in from the springhouse."

James thought, *When I said, 'Say no more,' I meant, 'Say no more.'*

As Delma walked away, she grinned and whispered to herself, *Now, if only I could find a sparrow in the rafters.*

Later, after settlin' on a yellow and gray checkered blanket, Charlotte waited while Delma filled out the sales ledger.

"Reckon he'll sleep tonight," she said.

Delma looked up with a puzzled look on her face.

Charlotte glanced at the far wall.

Following her gaze, Delma noticed the open window.

"Oh," she said with a smile. "Yes, I believe he will."

Both women giggled, being mindful that James couldn't overhear them.

As Mary looked through an impressive display of hair ribbons, Charlotte left through the front door.

"Bye, Charlotte," Mary called. "Hope Pauline enjoys her new blanket."

Charlotte waved.

"Delma, you think I could talk with you for a minute?" Mary asked as she handed over a shiny olive-green ribbon with strands of silver threads woven through it.

As Delma entered the ribbon into Pastor Wilson's account, she said, "Why of course you can, Mary."

"Outside?" asked Mary.

Delma looked at JJ where he laid in his playpen intently chewin' on the slobber smeared toes of his right foot.

"Okay," she said.

Throwin' a shawl and burp cloth over her shoulders, she reached down and picked up the baby.

"I'm takin' JJ out front for a minute," she called to James. "I'll be right back."

"Uh-uh," James grunted as he concentrated on driving a ten-penny nail into the hardwood plank wall without smashing his fingers. He'd never been handy with hammers and nails.

"Okay," Delma said, "let's go see what the menfolk find so captivatin' about them chairs out front."

After settlin' on the front porch with a cool breeze tousling errant strands of her long, loose hair, Delma looked both ways, up and down the Cove Road. Other than small wisps of powdery dust swirling about here and there, leavin' the roadside shrubbery uniformly coated in white, she saw no activity. No customers or passers-by were utilizing the rode. Unfastening a button on her bodice and strategically adjusting her shawl, she settled in to give JJ his lunch.

"So, what did you want to talk about?" she asked Mary.

Mary looked at her hands and fidgeted a bit as a

soft glow flushed her cheeks.

"I'm real sorry," she said. "I didn't mean to, but I just couldn't help overhear you and James talkin' outside the window." She glanced at Delma, then back at her lap.

"That's okay," Delma told Mary as she patted her arm. "Charlotte mentioned it too. I should have been more discreet when I talked to James. I'm sorry if it made you feel uncomfortable."

"No, it's not that at all," Mary said. "It's just that you seem to know how to talk to men. How they think."

Delma smiled. "Well, I don't know about that," she said. "Not all men are the same."

"Yeah, I know," said Mary. "I know there are good men, like my Pa, and Diver, and Mr. Banion too. And then there's them like that awful Mr. Haggen who kidnapped Billy and near got him killed."

She visibly shivered.

"It's just that I don't understand any of 'em."

JJ had finished feedin' so Delma placed him on the burp cloth on her shoulder and began softly pattin' and rubbin' his back.

"I don't really know what you're askin' me," she said. "Why don't you start over and tell me what you need to know."

Mary twisted a strand of golden hair around one finger and then another. She hesitated, not knowin' where to begin. Delma gave her arm a gentle squeeze and offered a friendly smile. Finally, Mary started by describin' her fight with Ally. The fight to prove my innocence.

"So, after my friends told me about Billy and Ally dancin' . . . Well, I was so mad I went and told Tyrone I'd go to the Harvest Festival with him."

JJ was layin' on the porch loosely wrapped in Delma's shawl. He was gigglin' as he tried to catch a cobbler moth as it fluttered around just out of reach.

"But you'd rather be goin' with Billy," Delma said.

Mary nodded her head without lookin' at Delma.

"I think I would," she said. She bit her lip. "But he hurt me bad."

Delma took both of Mary's hands.

"I know he did, dear," she said, "but I know Billy too. He'd never do anything to hurt you on purpose. It's just that he's so oblivious to the wiles of women,

61

he doesn't know when to nod and when to run."

Mary giggled as she thought about the first time she kissed me on the cheek. She wasn't sure if I was gonna pass out or if my ears were gonna catch fire.

"I know you're right," she told Delma. "But I don't know what to do. I can't tell Tyrone I'm not goin' with him. The hoe-down is this Saturday. It wouldn't be right after he's already made all the arrangements."

Delma brushed a strand of hair out of Mary's eyes and squeezed her shoulder. She so wanted to spare my feelings, but Mary was right.

"No, you can't, my dear," she said. "That wouldn't be fair. Tyrone did nothin' to deserve being treated that away. He should not be punished for you and Billy's misunderstanding."

Lookin' back to be sure JJ was doin' okay, she than took Mary's new ribbon from her hand and tied it in her hair.

"On the other hand, don't you think you should tell Billy how you feel. Let him know you're only going with Tyrone out of commitment."

Mary nodded. When she looked up her eyes were brimming with tears.

"Will he listen?" she asked. "Will he understand?"

Delma smiled. "If I know my little brother, he'll listen. He won't understand, but he'll listen, and more importantly, he'll wait. "For many years, Pa was a hard, hard man," she continued. "Few understood him. Fewer still, tried. Some even thought he'd lost his way. That is, until Diver came along anyway. But through it all, the one thing that never failed him was his sense of fairness. His sense of right and wrong. And above all things, that's what he passed along to his sons."

Mary looked deep into Delma's eyes. She so desperately wanted to believe every word she said.

"He is sweet," she said.
"Yes," said Delma. "He is sweet."

≈

I reckon some folks would say it just ain't fair that a fella could be born into a family like I got. Might even say I won the jackpot at birth. Well, I'd have to tell them folks, they might be right. But fair or not, they're my people and I ain't given up a one of 'em.

Mary took Delma's advice and rode Fancy up the

63

hill to explain why she had to go to the dance with Tyrone. It was tough, but I said I understood. She smiled at me and with a tear coursing down her cheek, gave me a kiss. Well, I'll tell ya now, that took a whole lot of the sting out of it. Seems funny how a little ol' peck on the cheek can brighten a fellas day, but it sure can.

Even Pa got somethin' out of my predicament. I was so desperate to take my mind off the dance, me and Baby spent the whole week huntin'. We took six coons, nine squirrels and one bobcat out of Pa's corn. What that bobcat was doing there, I don't know, but Pa was sure happy.

Ma later told me, when he didn't come in for his noontime meal, she took him some vitals out to his tannin' shed. Said she caught him doin' his own little hoedown as he worked them hides.

Kinda tickled me some is what it done.

FIVE

Cavalcade

THE HARVEST FESTIVAL HOEDOWN was being held at the Colby-Hannessy place in Dry Valley, about three miles south of Tuckaleechee Cove. The Colbys were cousins to the Becketts, and along with the Hannessys, the most prominent pig and sheep farmers in the region. Annually, Garrett Colby, the patriarch of the Colby-Hannessy clan would throw a hoedown primarily as a display of wealth, and to show that his cousin Orwell wasn't the only man of means in the mountains—not that Orwell ever felt that he and Garrett were in competition.

The rivalry, at least on Garrett's part, had apparently started between their fathers when Orwell's pa, being the older brother, received a larger inheritance than Garrett's pa. Garrett took the slight as a personal afront, birthright or no, and was determined to show he was every bit Orwell's equal.

Of course, he was far too frugal to sponsor a full-blown celebration like Orwell did every year on Independence Day, but he still felt his "everyone is welcome" annual hoedown showed his mettle.

The festivities were to begin with a feast at four, followed at five-thirty by the dance itself. With dusk falling at around six-thirty that time of year, the hoedown would wrap-up about an hour after dark. With folks from Tuckaleechee Cove having an hour's ride home and them from Cades Cove, two and a half or so, most everyone should make it home by ten and have time for evening chores before they turned in.

At one p.m. sharp, on the day of the dance, Tyrone and Susan pulled up in front of Pastor Wilson's clapboard cottage. It was a well-kept, pretty little bungalow, nestled in a pine grove about a mile east of the Baptist Church. As was Tyrone's practice, he estimated its perceived value compared to that of his father's home and found it wanting.

A robin loosed a mumbled *tuk-tuk-tuk*, from her nest high in the treetops while a couple of energetic

66

fox squirrels stirred up a racket scampering about in the carpet of fallen pinecones and needles. Every few minutes they would dash up a towering tree trunk and race 'round and around as stealthily as if still on level ground—claws clattering on the rough bark. Then, back down again, and through the leaf litter along the roadways edge. They never seemed to tire in their endless game of chase.

Only when Susan climbed down from the high-gloss buggy and hurried to the cottage door did they pause in their play. Hiding on the backside of a tree, the occasional flick of a fluffy red tail or swivel of a pointy ear were the only signs to betray their refuge.

Tyrone remained sitting on the padded seat of his buggy's lazy-back bench, keepin' a tight rein on the spirited blood bay mare.

Pastor Wilson answered the door.

"Hello, Susan," he said. "You're lookin' mighty pretty today."

Susan giggled as she bounced her hanging curls with upturned palms. "Momma did my hair," she said. She then gave a practiced curtsy.

Wilson laughed and gave a stiff bow. "Mary's in

her room. Go on in."

As Susan hurried into Mary's room, Wilson strolled out to talk with Tyrone.

"Looks like a fine day," he said, observing the clear blue sky.

"Yes, sir," Tyrone said, sittin' a bit straighter and runnin' a hand through his wind tousled hair, "'bout as fine a day as a fella could ask for."

"And a fine horse and buggy ya got here too," Pastor Wilson said as he ran his hand over the smooth master-crafted woodwork.

"Ain't another like it in the Cove," beamed Tyrone.

"I should think not," said the pastor.

The horse stamped a foot, swished her tail, and neighed as if in agreement.

Tyrone's chest swelled and a smile of pride lit his face. He raised his chin and grasped his suspender's strap, acknowledging the praise.

"Yes siree," said the pastor, "With a fine day like this and a magnificent rig like that, I don't reckon there's any reason at all that my daughter won't be home by ten . . . do you?"

"No, sir," said Tyrone, his shoulders slumping.

Ten o'clock should have been the soonest. With any luck, he'd planned to drop Susan off on the way home, claiming he needed to take care of the horse and buggy. That would have given him and Mary some 'alone time'.

But, like a master chessman, the pastor had stymied his plans without him even seeing it coming.

Got to give it to him, he thought. *I walked right into that one. What was it that Pastor Steadman often quoted from Proverbs. . . "Pride goeth before destruction, and a haughty spirit before a fall*?"

Tyrone had just learned that lesson firsthand, but being one who relished havin' the last word, he upped the ante with, "I wouldn't be a bit surprised if she ain't home even sooner."

Even as the words left his mouth, he paled and bit his tongue. *What was that*? he thought.

"Fine. Fine," said Pastor Wilson as he patted Tyrone on the knee. "I'm glad we read the weather the same way."

"Yes, sir, Pastor," said Tyrone. *But she's mine till then,* he thought.

The front door flew open, and Mary followed Susan out of the cottage. Susan was nearly skipping; she was so excited.

"We're gonna have such fun," she gushed as she waved to Pastor Wilson on her way to the buggy. "I can't wait to get there."

Pastor Wilson took Mary's hands as she paused before him. *So much like a woman. Where has the time gone?* he thought. He smiled down at her.

"You have a wonderful time," he said.

Then kissing her on the cheek, he stood back and lovingly straightened her sun hat, adjusting the slightly crooked bow beneath her chin.

"You look as pretty as your mother," he said.

Mary saw him swallow a lump in his throat.

"She'd be so proud."

Mary's eyes clouded. "Thanks, Pa," she said.

Then loud enough for Tyrone to hear, the pastor said, "I'll be looking for you around nine-thirty."

"Nine-thirty?" questioned Mary. "I thought the ride from Dry Valley would take at least till ten."

"As did I," said the Pastor, "but young Master Beckett assured me he can make the trip sooner. Now, go on with ya."

Tyrone moaned.

The bay whinnied.

Pastor Wilson grinned.

"Well, better be on your way," he said. "I saw Casey and his bunch go by in Diver's carriage about a quarter hour ago".

Mary hurried to the buggy, then to Tyrone's dismay, waited for Susan to climb up first, placing her between him and his date.

As Susan settled on the soft leather bench, she reached down to help Mary up and winked. The seating arrangements had been worked out between them before they'd left Mary's room.

"Away, my good man," Susan quipped to Tyrone with an exaggerated British accent. "The ladies would go to the ball."

The girls laughed as Tyrone rolled his eyes. He then nodded to Wilson and with a snap of the reins, they were off.

"Tallyho!" called Susan as she and Mary both waved a farewell to Pastor Wilson. "Good night, good sir, good night. Though parting is such sweet sorrow, we must bid thee good night till it be morrow."

Mary snorted as she took Susan's arm in hers, then reached up to place a hand on top her hat. Both girls pealed with laughter, forcing even Tyrone to grin. Though things were not workin' out quite as he had envisioned them, they looked to have a joyous ride ahead of them all the same. And with two and a half hours to travel, the possibilities were endless.

Arriving at the lower slope of Rich Mountain Road, they soon settled in with a small convoy of seven assorted wagons and carriages along with three riders on horseback, all makin' the festive trip. The conveyances were pulled by everything from long eared plow mules to massive draft horses, none of which, Tyrone concluded, held a candle to the noble bearing of his very own blood bay mare.

As the procession got underway many drivers cheered and doffed their hats, calling back and forth with outlandish claims of personal prowess on the dance floor and making playful jibes at the stumblin' attempts of others. The favorite topic was the retellin' of how Rolf Schmitt unknowingly blew out the seat of his britches while demonstrating an old German dance step at Orwell's Fourth of July celebration. The bright red glare of his newly purchased union suit contrasting with the backside of his charcoal trousers sent the gathered men into convulsions of laughter, while half the womenfolk of the Cove succumbed to a heavy case of the flutters.

Rolf, thinkin' the jovial buffoonery was encouragement of his performance, had become even more animated. He'd throwin' his arms wide and kicking ever higher with each dance step he took. A massive smile beamed from his face, and he was having the time of his life all the way up until his wife, Jenny, came rushin' through the crowd and threw a blanket around his waist.

Laughter rolled across the peaks and hollows of the misty hills and a cheer sent birds to flight as Rolf gingerly rose from the seat of his lumber wagon and tipped his hat. His thinning blond, Bavarian hair, did little to hide his bright red scalp as if demonstratin' to one and all the very shade and color of which they spoke.

"Sit down!" Jenny chided as she tugged on his Linsey-Woolsey, home-spun shirt. Her face glowed scarlet with an intensity that would have driven a proud male cardinal out of the mountains in shame.

As he settled, she covered her face with both hands and howled with embarrassed laugher 'til tears streamed from her eyes.

Dean and Lidia, along with Casey and Thelma, joined in the merriment as they followed the Schmitts in Diver's borrowed carriage. Everyone knew the stout German was the first to enjoy a joke, even if the jibe was pointed his way.

Soon, the hilarity settled down and the chucklin' ceased. Only the clattering, squeaking, clanking ruckus of iron wheels on jostlin' wagons disturbed the solitude of the mountains. With each switchback and new rise, the horses snorted and flicked their tails as they drove their mighty shoulders and broad chests into the sweaty harnesses.

Then, with the vaporous mist clearing, and the thick foliage falling away on the north side of the trail, a breathtaking view opened up before the eyes of the travelers.

"Aahs," could be heard as each lumbering conveyance passed before the scene.

Far below, a vast expanse of scattered farms, cultivated fields, and peacefully feeding livestock stretched out like a giant tapestry woven across the landscape to merge with the shadows of the purple hills beyond. A sliver of silver sunlight sparkled off the gently flowing waters of Abrams Creek as it rippled over the occasional, shallow cascade on its way across the fertile valley. A gang of neighborhood kids could be seen enthusiastically jumping off the wooden railing of a farm access bridge before splashin' down in the crystal-clear water, then clambering back up the muddy bank to hurriedly get in line to leap again.

No doubt they were having a boisterous time though no sound could be heard at that distance.

Nestled in the midst of the picturesque valley landscape, seemingly framed by two deep groves of broad chestnut oak trees and tall straight pines, stood the shimmering white clapboard walls of the Cades Cove Baptist Church. A steep-roofed bell tower stood perched atop its shake shingled roofline, like an angel adorning a Christmas tree.

Someone, probably Mr. Blyth, was sweepin' the front steps in preparation for the next day's service while a doe and two yearlings snacked on the tender grasses behind the small cemetery.

As the last wagon passed beyond the overlook, Jas Deerborn who had been applying a fresh coat of rosin on his bow, drew it across his fiddle strings creating a clear high-pitched screech that soon transformed into a fast tempo tune.

Turkey in the Straw, someone yelled. And in an instant, Thelma's pretty alto voice filled the air.

> As I was a goin' on down the road,
> Had a tired team and a heavy load,
> I cracked my whip and the leader sprung,
> I said good day to my wagon tongue.

Everyone laughed. The lyrics weren't perfect, but close enough. They all joined in on the chorus, then followed Thelma into another verse.

> I went to milkin' but didn't know how,
> I milked the goat instead of the cow,
> A monkey was sittin' on a pile of straw,
> He's just a-winkin' at his mother-in-law.

Turkey in the straw, turkey in the hay,
Turkey in the straw, what do ya say . . .

That opened the floodgates. Someone called for
Home, Sweet Home, another for *The Old Oaken
Bucket*. Lidia Tudwell requested her Uncle Pierre's
favorite, *Au Clair De La Lune* (By the Light of the
Moon.)

Laughter, song, and merriment filled the hills.
Irish, Scotch, Brits, and Hessians, each rode with
pride alongside their companions. Old allegiances and
cultural differences were washed away and relegated
to a bygone era. These brave, industrious, strong-
backed mountain folk, had cleared a wilderness, tilled
the land, and built a community together. They were
friends, confidantes, and neighbors. They were
Americans, one and all.

Gradually, the gaiety wavered and settled down
into less boisterous conversations between travelin'
companions. The astonishing pallet of fall colors
displayed by each new hollow or sun-lit mountain
slope sent thrills of delight through the hearts of the

young ladies, and dreams of future homesteads through that of the men. An occasional chill drifted on the wind as spring-fed cascades washing down bare-rock precipices flowed in shallow rivulets across the narrow road. Errant gusts of wayward wind caused shrieks of astonishment and startled peals of laughter as they doused unsuspecting travelers with frigid mist drifting off the nearby falls.

"There's a couple blankets in the boot locker," Tyrone said.

The girls scrambled to open the small trunk behind the seat and retrieve the blankets before they reached the icy breeze.

Tyrone noticed he was left to fend for himself.

Miles passed beneath rock polished wagon wheels and iron-shod hooves. Narrow passages clung to steep, wooded slopes, eliciting nervous glances and white knuckled shrieks from the womenfolk. In the distant, beautiful mountain vistas peaked between lofty hilltops before the trail dropped into wide, brushy valleys strewn with clearwater streams.

As Mary and Susan speculated on who would get the most dance requests at the hoedown, they lost track of their whereabouts and didn't notice when Rich Mountain Road merged with the old Lion's Den Camp Trail.

Lion's Den, named after an old panther's lair, sheltered under the crag of a cliff, was a long-abandoned hunter's encampment that Joseph Dula had tried to develop into a thriving community. He'd led four trusting, down-on-their-luck dirt farmers from Southern Pennsylvania to the camp, along with their families, with the promise of endless valleys deep in fertile soil, and wide-open forests and streams teaming with fish and game.

To show his good faith in the venture, he'd even agreed to swap, acre-for-acre, his mountain paradise for the deed to their worn-out Pennsylvania holdings.

"They couldn't lose."

After two years of unusually harsh winters: thin, rocky, hardscrabble soil that could barely produce enough cornmill nubbins to feed their families even when heavily augmented with cattail-root flour, and woodlands that had been overhunted for years, the farmers could do nothing but concede defeat.

By then, even their Pennsylvania dirt farms had

been sold.

The old Lion's Den Camp Trail was now seldom used, and would soon revert back to the thick, dark woodlands it had been cut from.

Three more miles, and one last switchback, saw Rich Mountain Road widened into a long sweeping descent. Far in the distance, two mountain balds and numerous wide-open fields were dotted with scattered flocks of feeding sheep.

"Look!" shouted Susan as she grabbed Mary's arm and pointed. "I think I see your little lamb."

Mary laughed at the mention of Sarah Hale's nursery rhyme. Miss Shelly had spent an entire day teaching it to the class so they could recite it for their parents.

The jovial feeling didn't last long. As the travelers continued down the slope, they entered the valley proper and were soon struck by a strong, pungent odor that nearly overwhelmed their senses. Gagging and pinching their noses, they looked out across the lowlands on either side of the road. Hundreds of bristle-backed hogs were rooting through the muddy fields. Thirty acres had been uprooted and turned under as effectively as if by a mule team and plow.

"Eewww," Susan moaned, a blanket stuffed tight against her face. "That smells even worse than when you take your shoes off, Tyrone."

Tyrone reddened.

Mary, holding her nose and covering her mouth, looked the other way so Tyrone wouldn't see her grin.

Leave it to Susan, Tyrone thought. *The one person in the world I can't thump in front of Mary.*

As the wagons climbed the incline up to the Colby-Hannessy farms, the porcine odor faded. Up ahead, near a massive, open-sided barn, sat a dozen or so horse-drawn rigs. They'd arrived at the Garrett's Tuckaleechee Harvest Festival Hoedown.

SIX

If It's Meant To Be

A S YOU CAN IMAGINE, on the day of the dance, I was a mess. I didn't know if I should go huntin', or fishin', or visitin' with Diver or Delma, or maybe just lay in my loft and reread one of the three dog-eared books I was soon gonna have to take back to Miss Shelly.

As I dawdled around the homeplace, idly kicking sticks into the underbrush that Baby hurriedly fetched and dropped back under foot, I heard a tapping coming from Pa's tanning shed. Going over to investigate, I saw Pa standing inside with the door propped open, diligently tacking a hide to a scraping frame in preparation of fleshing it.

"Yo, Pa," I said. "Mind if I watch?"

"Not at all, Son," he replied.

I'm sure he was a bit taken aback, seein's how I'd never taken much interest when he preserved hides before.

I picked up a thumb-sized piece of cedar, and pulling my straight knife, settled in on the tannin' shed porch to do some whittling. Baby sniffed around at my fragrant shavings a bit, then ambled off toward the creek to find more interesting entertainment.

"So, what ya up to?" Pa asked as he looked over his Indian style bone scrapers, selecting the best one for the task ahead.

"Aw, nothin'," I said.

Pa raised an eyebrow as he grasped the handle of his scraper with his right hand and placed the heel of his left palm slightly above it to create the right friction for fleshing without damaging the green pelt.

"Way your Ma tells it, your gal's goin' floor stompin' without ya today."

I took an unintended chunk out of my whittle stick.

"Yeah, I messed up some, though I ain't rightly figured out what I done," I said. "Then she up and told Tyrone Beckett she'd go to the dance with him."

Pa simply nodded.

I sliced another long sliver out of my stick. I meant to that time.

"She later said she'd rather be goin' with me, but kinda felt obligated to him after givin' her word and all."

Pa worked in silence for a few moments creating a small fleshless patch on the hairless underside of the hide which he then began expanding downward.

"Reckon so," Pa said. "A gal that'll stand by her word even when it ain't convenient to do so, is a gal worth her salt."

I held my stick out at arm's length to eyeball it for straightness then trimmed back a small knob.

"Ain't easy though," I said.

What I was really thinkin' was, *I reckon if Ma had done such a thing, there'd be one less fella walkin' 'round with his scalp on tight.*

"No, sir," Pa said. "'Tain't easy, but if it's truly meant to be, these things have a way of workin' themselves out."

I reckoned Pa was right, but it somehow didn't do much to ease the hollow feelin' I had deep in my innards.

After a moment of silence, Pa straightened up to work a kink out of his back and flick gummy chunks of clinging flesh off the tip of his scraper. He looked down at me.

"You ever heard of the Hessians?" he asked.

"Yes, sir," I said. "According to Miss Shelly, they were an army of German soldiers from the state of Hesse-Kassel that the British hired to fight our colonials during the War of Independence."

"That's right," he said. "They were a mighty tough bunch. And disciplined too. They were well-paid, well-trained, and well outfitted professional fightin' men. And they were led by officers who gained their rank through merit . . . not pedigree. Men that any soldier would be proud to follow.

"Unfortunately, being men of no standin' back home—what many considered 'vermin' or 'expendable' they often delved into low and despicable acts of brutality. With the approval of a few deviant officers . . . though officially it was forbidden (or as a fur trader I used to deal with liked to say, *verboten*') they eagerly pillaged remote homesteads and settlements to supplement their income, and quite often tormented their helpless prisoners.

"As you might imagine, they were despised above all others by the colonial militias and backwoods settlers alike. Many a man, be he loyalist or rebel, turned his back on the King because of the Hessians."

Pa readjusted his fleshing frame, then continued his tale.

"As it so happened, there was one young Hessian grenadier by the name of Tobias Krause, who not only refused to join his comrades in their barbarous acts but did all he could to try and protect as many innocent noncombatants as possible. He pleaded for decency and urged his fellow soldiers to think of their own families back home.

"'What if someone treated them this way?'

"At great personal risk to himself and his career, he lodged an official protest with his commanding officers—believing it would force them to make some changes.

"All for naught. The atrocities continued and Tobias received double assignments of nighttime sentry duty."

Pa set the sturdy fleshing frame aside and began meticulously cleaning his scrapers. He then brushed off his leather apron.

I sat holdin' my forgotten whittle stick, waiting for him to continue his story.

"Well," he said, inspecting the hide one last time, "the war finally ended, and most of the Hessians went home. But a few had come to admire this new land; its endless forests, crystal waters, and brave, strong inhabitants. They were determined to plant roots and carve out a home of their own.

"Rememberin' the good-natured grenadier and the kindness he had shown his prisoners, the wilderness settlers encouraged him to stay and welcomed him with open arms.

"All, that is, except a down-on-his-luck farmer by the name of Nate Crowder. Nate had lost a brother and an uncle to the 'Hessian heathens', and he said he'd see every last one of 'em laid low before he'd welcome them to be his neighbor."

By this time, I had no idea where Pa was headed with his story, but it was the most I'd heard the man say in fifteen years and you couldn't have pried me off that porch with a fifty-pound keg of Mr. du Pont's Brandywine River Blasting Powder.

You might say, I was interested.

"As luck would have it," Pa continued, "Tobias stayed and got a job as a gardener and hunter for the *Hound & Horn Tavern* in Schuylerville, New York. That's where he first met Mitzy Sue Crowder, Nate's oldest daughter, who had come into town looking to have her spinning wheel's flyer axel repaired.

"Mitzy stopped Tobias on the street to ask directions to the nearest blacksmith shop. Being instantly smitten, instead of directing her, he escorted her. And after that, he showed her about town, treated her to a meal at the *Hound & Horn Tavern*, and even showed her his favorite "lazy day" get-a-way on the banks of the Hudson River. In no time at all, the young couple were hopelessly in love.

"Of course, Nate was having none of it. No plea, promise or petition from the young couple would sway his mind. No Hessian would ever marry his daughter. Tobias went as far as to offer five years of servitude for Mitzy's hand.

"Nate replied by cocking a musket.

"Mitzy, being a resolute and loving daughter, would never dream of disobeying her father's wishes, though tears streamed as she hung her head and submitted to his will.

"'It cannot be,' she told Tobias as she hugged him tightly. "Though I vow with all my heart, I will never marry another.'

"That night, Tobias left Schuylerville to join a troupe of militia led by Capt. Lawrence Moore in pursuit of a band of young Iroquois warriors who had been harassing outlying homesteads. The campaign consisted mainly of traversing rocky peaks and sloshing through tangled marshes in an uninhabited region northeast of the Hudson River headwaters. No contact was made between the combatants, and the only casualties or bloodletting was due to sprained ancles and painful, honey locust thorns. After three months of pursuit, the warriors disbanded, and the settlers returned home. All, that is, except Tobias. As his comrades turned south, Tobias continued west. He visited the massive falls called Niagara, spent a winter sheltered in snows so deep a moose would have floundered in them, and marveled at the great freshwater seas called lakes. He fought bears and wolves and lost his right moccasin to an angry badger. Surveyed endless miles of majestic forests and slogged through impenetrable swamps.

"While Tobias trekked, Mitzy Sue waited, and Nate's fortunes grew. Bein' a man strongly suspected of underhanded dealings; he had acquired a nice piece of bottom land on the Sweet Water branch of the Hudson River. About as fertile a section as the valley offered. Rowdy Slater, the settler who had cleared the tilled and site fiercely protested, but Nate produced a dubious script signed by Major Benjamin Tallmadge of Washington's Continental Army deeding the property to him. Refusing to delay taking possession, Nate even took the man's crops.

"The only thing he desired, that he didn't have, was grandchildren. His oldest son was married, but had produced no heirs, and Mitzy, having promised Tobias she'd stay single forever, planned to keep her oath. His other two daughters and youngest boy were not yet of age.

"Even as Nate's wealth grew, and his reputation dwindled, young Tobias Krause was busy building a homestead of his own. He had settled on land granted him by Chief Little Turtle of the Miami Tribe. It was nestled in a fertile stretch of towering pines along the southern shores of the lake known as Lac des Illinois, by the French; Michi gami, by the Ojibwe; and Michigan, by the Americans. He and the chief had been allies and close friends during the American Revolution and Little Turtle had offered him refuge if he ever desired it.

"One night as Tobias sat cross-legged before a crackling campfire with a Potawatomi friend and his new bride, looking up at the expanse of God's great creation, a calmness settled over his soul. A calmness he hadn't even realized he'd been lacking.

"The multitude of brilliant stars nestled in the endless night sky was the same he had so often marveled at when just a child back on the banks of the Fulda River in Germany. He suddenly had a desire to go home. But to his amazement, it wasn't the home of his childhood that he missed. It was his new, adopted home. After two years, his westward trek was over."

As Pa talked, he'd been unpegging his hide. He then turned it skin side out and slowly immersed it into a trough of warm water.

"That should do it," he said. "We'll let it soak a couple days to loosen the membrane, and then scrape it down again."

Placin' a large rock on the sodden hide to keep it submerged, he dried his hands before continuing his story.

"It was a long haul back to the settlements," he said, "but Tobias made good time. Now and again, he had to skirt native villages, but bein' well versed in wilderness travel, he easily avoided any unwanted confrontations. Even his friendship with Little Turtle couldn't guarantee his acceptance with every member of the Six Nations.

"Finally, on a crisp April morning, just after sunrise, as he was makin' his way along the banks of a Hudson River tributary, he heard white men's voices. But not just any voices. They were the harsh voices of an angry mob.

"Pushin' through the underbrush, he entered the clearing of a well-appointed homestead. A two-story cabin and cantilever barn were nestled among several acres of rich, black soil awaiting springs first furrow.

92

In the doorway of the cabin, a shirtless man stood, musket in hand before the angry mob. The muzzle of a second musket protruded from the shooting port of a shuttered window.

"'I got a signed declaration right here from Major Tallmadge himself,' declared a bushy-faced man at the head of the mob. He waved a sheet of parchment over his head. 'It disavows him ever granting land in the Hudson Valley to any man, and on top of that, he says he's never even heard the name, Nate Crowder.'

"The crowd roared, and the man in the doorway backed up a step as he raised his musket.

"*Nate Crowder*? thought Tobias. When he'd left on his travels, the Crowder homestead was nowhere near these parts.

"'Is ya comin' out or is we comin' in to get ya?' cried the leader.

"'I say we hang him!' shouted someone in the crowd.

"'Why waist a good rope?' someone else bellowed. 'I say we burn him out!'

"'Whoa, now boys!' the leader called as he raised both arms and turned to face the crowd. 'Ain't nobody gonna burn my cabin.'

"Tobias, hearin' feminine pleas from inside the cabin, stepped forward and addressed the man with the parchment.

"'What's the problem here?' he asked.

"The man stared at Tobias suspiciously. He didn't know what the stranger had to do with this business, but on the other hand, he didn't look like one to be trifled with either.

"'My name's Rowdy Slater,' he said, 'and that fella there,' he pointed at Nate, 'stole my property, claimin' it was given him by Major Tallmadge of the Continental Army.'

"He thrust the parchment in Tobias' face.

"'I got proof right here that he lied.'

"Tobias took the sheet and read it. He then rolled it up and handed it back to Rowdy.

"'Okay, Mr. Slater,' he said, 'Let's say your letter is the real thing.'

"'Ain't nothin' but,' declared Rowdy.

"'If I could convince Mr. Crowder to vacate the premises,' continued Tobias, 'would you let him leave peacefully?'

94

"A grumble arose from the crowd.

"'This ... vacate thing?' said Rowdy, tuggin' at his beard. 'That mean he'd be gettin' off my land?'

"'Yes, it does,' stated Tobias.

"'Ain't got no right to walk free,' someone yelled.

"'I still say we hang him,' someone else called.

"A cheer arose from the crowd.

"'Now, hold on there,' Rowdy shouted out above the din. 'All I'm askin' is that the man take his family and get gone. I ain't lookin' for no hangin'.'

"As the noise lowered to a discontented grumble, Rowdy turned back to Tobias. 'You get him off my property and he can go,' he said. 'I'll give him till noon tomorrow. That's more 'n he gave me."

Pa finished puttin' up his scrapin' tools then slapped me on the back and said, "Reckon Ma outta have lunch about ready."

"But, Pa," I said as we exited the tannin' shed, "how'd Tobias get Nate to leave?"

"He offered him his homestead on the big lake," he said.

"His own homestead?" I blurted.

"Yep," Pa said. "And all he asked in return was

Mitzy Sue's hand.

"Mitzy, herself had been hidden in the cabin throughout the entire confrontation and had no idea who'd interceded for her pa. All she knew was somebody had asked for her hand, and her pa had accepted. He knew good and well she'd vowed to never marry! Rushin' to the door in a panic, she burst out into the open and stopped. For an instant she was froze in place. Standing there with a big grin on his face was no other than her young Hessian Grenadier. The savior of her family was Tobias himself. Well, I'll tell ya, Son, she wasn't about to let her pa outta that one. Tobias had given up everything he owned, but he'd come for her at last. They could always start over. This time together.

Pa closed the door and shoved home the locking peg.

"It wasn't easy, mind you," he said, "but I reckon them young'uns just weren't willin' to be parted ever again."

He then brushed back his greying hair with his left hand before replacing his cap with his right. A slight adjustment, and he seemed to think it was sittin' proper.

"Yep, I reckon it must have been a mighty fine thing, makin' ol' Nate eat his words," Pa said with a chuckle. "Come harvest time them young folks got hitched." He winked at me. "So, like I told ya before, if it's to be, it'll be."

To tell ya the truth, I'd plumb forgotten why Pa had been tellin' me the story in the first place. But upon reflection, I reckoned he was probably right.

"Still, what happened to Tobias and Mitzy?" I asked him. "Ya can't just end the story by sayin' they got together."

Pa laughed.

"Well, they lived a nice long life," he said. "A lot longer than Nate did. He tried his shenanigans with the Miami's, and it didn't go so well. For the sake of Tobias and his bride, Little Turtle allowed Nate's family to return east, but Nate himself is lying in a shallow grave somewhere on the shores of Lake Michigan.

"Anyway, Mitzy gave Tobias a whole passel of young'uns. When he eventually passed away, his youngest daughter; a girl they called Gertrude, was

97

still unwed. Needin' a home of her own, she married an older widower by the name of Hans von der Schmitt. As it turned out, that was a pretty good move too. Though it started as a marriage of convenience, what with him havin' several years on her, he was a good man. It wasn't long before they fell in love for true. Folks said they never saw a more devoted couple. They even had a son. A fine, strong, strappin' young fella of the finest character."

Pa grinned. "Now, if you want to know *his* story, you can just amble on down there to the sawmill and ask him for yourself. They named him Rudolph Tobias Schmitt. Course, we just call him Rolf."

SEVEN

One-eighty Proof

A S THE CARAVAN FROM Cades Cove rattled onto the Colby-Hannessy homestead, a tow-headed boy of perhaps ten or twelve years old pointed out a small pasture of good thick grass for them to park on. No sooner had they scattered across the greenery then a gaggle of laughing, huffing youngins came sloshing over to each conveyance with a bucket of water for their horses.

"Ol' Garrett's goin' all out this year," somebody said, and set folks to chucklin'.

The men tied back their brakes, hobbled their horses, or attached ground anchors to halters before coming 'round to help the women folk down from the wagons.

Tyrone, tryin' hard to impress Mary with his

chivalrous side, had no more than helped her down to terra firma when he was suddenly attacked from behind by two wildly yelpin' and whoppin' young men. It happened so quickly; Mary barely had time to jump out of the way. She gasped as she yanked her new dress clear of the fray before it got soiled and tattered.

The miscreants all went crashin' to the ground under the buggy, instantly punchin' and spittin' and bitin' and rollin' 'round like rabid wildcats fightin' over a choice peace of rancid fatback.

The blood bay mare didn't like it a bit and reared up as she whinnied; wild-eyed and blowin'. She would have run if Tyrone hadn't both, tied the brake back, and fastened her to a heavy anchor. Even at that, the buggy violently jerked about as Susan was trying to climb down on her own. In an instant, she was tumbling, bloomers over bonnet, to the ground.

"Are you alright?" cried Mary as she rushed over to help Susan to her feet.

"I'm a sight better off than these brain-dead knuckleheads are gonna be when I'm done with 'em," she hissed.

She ran over and began viciously kicking every exposed body part she could reach as it presented itself; be it ribcage, shin bone, or forehead.

"Ow! . . . ow! . . . OW!" they screamed.

Scattering, the boys climbed out from under the far side of the buggy. Tyrone came around and stood near Mary, red faced and embarrassed. The other two looked on from the far side of the conveyance, wisely keeping it between themselves and Susan.

"This is our cousins, Gary Colby and Trey Hannessy," Susan told Mary. "Ain't never been two more useless critters ever walked the back country— or anywhere else, as far as I know."

Gary and Trey looked at each other and grinned.

"You gonna let her talk that away 'bout yer own kinfolk?" Gary asked Tyrone.

"I surely wouldn't," Tyrone said, "if it weren't true. Ha!" he laughed.

"Yeah? Well!" Trey sputtered. "Well . . ."

He stood blank faced and puzzled. He never had acquired the flair for a snappy comeback. Sometimes he'd wake in the middle of the night, blarin' out a zinger for a spat that had happened hours before.

"Don't hurt yerself, cous'," Gary laughed as he looked into Trey's searching eyes.

All three boys broke out into peals of laughter.

"So, they're not mad at Tyrone?" Mary asked Susan.

"No," said Susan with a smirk and a shake of her head. "That's how they say 'hey.'"

"Well, they sure had me fooled," said Mary.

"Hee, hee," chuckled Tyrone as he brushed off his best outfit. "Come on over here boys. I want ya to meet my gal."

Mary blanched. She'd told Tyrone she'd go to the hoedown with him, but she certainly had *not* said she was his girl.

"Mary," Tyrone said as he half bowed and swept his open hand out towards the grass-stained and snickering pair. "This is Gary and Trey. Fact is, no matter what Susan says, they're pretty good old boys."

He then put his arm 'round Mary's shoulder. "Boys," he said, "this is my date, Mary."

Mary immediately shrugged his hand off her shoulder and stepped away. Susan stepped between them.

The cousins snickered. "Mary," they said in unison as they stretched out their right arms and bowed at the waist like Sir Raleigh before Queen Elizabeth.

"Boys," Mary said, reaching down and grasping Susan's hand.

Tyrone stood red-faced and glowering.

A clanging sound erupted from a nearby clearing.

"Sounds like the feast is ready," piped in Susan. "Come on Mary. Let's hurry so we can find a good seat."

As the girls rushed away, Gary and Trey came 'round the buggy to stand by Tyrone.

"Looks like there's a fly in the ointment," Garry said with a snicker.

Tyrone flashed him the stink eye, then glanced over to watch Mary and Susan disappear into the crowd.

"Ain't nothin' I can't fix before I take her home tonight," he mumbled as he thumbed his suspender's straps and puffed out his chest. *If I can get rid of Susan*, he thought.

"We got somethin' that'll cheer ya up, one way or

t' other," Gary said.

"Yes, we do," agreed Trey with a big, crooked grin on his face.

Tyrone looked back at his cousins. "Yeah, what's that?" he asked.

"Well," Gary began with a smirk on his face, "Ma was all worked up over losin' a jug o' spicy apple butter preserves to a saggin' self-board in the springhouse..."

"Nasty stuff, if ya ask me," cut in Trey.

"So, Pa told me and Trey to clean up the mess and replace the board."

Shakin' his head, Trey said, "He told Gary to do it, is what he done, I only got dragged into it 'cause I happened to be there at the time."

A muscle flinched in Gary's jaw as he eyed his cousin. His right hand tightened into a fist.

"Anyway," Gary continued, "we were clearing out the canned goods to make way for the new board . . .

"And we come across a jug of Uncle Freddy's corn squeezin's," blurted out Trey.

Garry whipped off his hat and hit Trey upside the head with it.

104

"Ow!" cried Trey, rubbin' his reddening face. "What'd you do that for."

"I was tellin' the story," said Gary.

"Well then, go ahead and tell it," Trey said.

Turning back to Tyrone, Gary said, "Like I was sayin', we was . . ." He stopped with a puzzled look on his face. Then looking back at Trey, he said, "You done told him. How am I gonna tell him after you done did it?"

"I got the picture, boys," Tyrone said before the ruckus evolved into fisticuffs. "Y'all found a jug of Uncle Freddy's moonshine in the springhouse." Tyrone grinned. "Folks say there ain't nobody can cook corn squeezin's like Uncle Freddy can. Where is it?"

Garry and Trey looked at each other and smiled.

"Follow us!" they shouted in unison. Then turning, they raced across the yard; shoving, and kicking as they went.

Tyrone stood grinning and shaking his head for a moment. "Dingbats," he said. Then pressing his hat down tight, he took up the chase.

≈

While the cousins hurried off to do what teenaged boys will do, Mary and Susan were enjoying the dance. They stood with a small group of giggling gals, clapping to the music, and cheering on the swirling participants. It wasn't long before they were invited to join in the fun by a couple of handsome youths who had ridden in from Tuckaleechee Cove.

The evening was cool, the music was lively, and the polite young men managed to make it through a complete quadrille without stepping on either Mary or Susan's toes. Everyone was having a great time and the missing cousins were long forgotten.

"Can I get ya some punch?" Larry asked Mary as they stepped from the dance floor making way for another couple.

"Thank you," said Mary. "I'd love some."

"Me too," said Susan to her dance partner, Les, before he had time to ask . . . *or not.*

The two buddies hurried off towards the refreshment table, elbowing each other and joking as they went.

"They're nice," said Mary.

"Yeah, but I don't think Chance or Billy would think so," quipped Susan.

"Ha, I have no doubt of it," Mary laughed. "But it serves 'em right for not being here," she said. "Billy for lettin' that Alley girl buffalo him the way she done, and Chance for not findin' somebody else to help out his Ma for one night."

"Why, Mary," Susan said with a feigned look of shock on her face, "I think I'm rubbing off on you."

Mary laughed.

The evening slipped away far too quickly, interspersed with song and dance and good companionship. Lanterns were lit and hung from the rafters making the open-sided barn glow like a beacon in the gathering dark. A cool, damp fog drifted into the low-lying swine-fields where it swirled and billowed and slowing advanced up the hillside. All to soon, Cat Eye McGarity, lookin' a bit winded but as jolly as ever, announced the last dance.

"Sounds like it's my turn."

Mary spun around to find Tyrone standing right

behind her. She didn't know why, but he seemed to be swaying on his feet; and unless it was a trick of the lantern-light, his eyes looked wet and bloodshot.

He used the back of his hand to wipe a line of spittle from the corner of his mouth.

"Come on Mary," he slurred, "let's show 'em how it's done."

As the musicians tuned up for the last reel and folks shuffled onto the floor, he grabbed her by the hand with a sharp yank that nearly tumbled her to the floor.

"Ow," Mary said. "That hurt."

Mary suddenly found herself standing amongst the other dancers facing a leering Tyrone. By the twinge she felt in her shoulder, she had no doubt she'd be bruised come morning. If it weren't for the fact that she'd come to the hoe-down with him, she would have turned around right then and there and left him standing on the dance floor by himself.

She glanced over to where Susan had been watching only to see the back of the girl's head as she slipped through the crowd.

"So much for a chaperone," she thought.

Wishing she could go with Susan, she instead steeled her resolve to get through the next few minutes with as little pain as possible. She figured she owed Tyrone at least one dance.

Tyrone chuckled as he bowed to Mary.

"Whew!" she said. "What's that smell?"

Tyrone's face blanched.

"Oh," he said. "I guess the wind's picking up off the hog pens."

"That don't smell like any hogs I ever been around," she said.

Tyrone snickered, then belched.

The sudden expulsion of twice-distilled, one-eighty proof, pure grain alcohol, directly into her face made Mary gag and her eyes water.

She didn't even get the chance to catch her breath before the music started and Tyrone grabbed her hands pulling her around the floor.

"Swing your partner . . ." called Cat Eye.

Tyrone grabbed Mary around the waist with one arm and drew her up tight to him.

She turned her head as far as she could, gasping for clean air. At the same time, Tyrone began high stepping and "Yee-hawing," as he spun her around the room.

She fought desperately trying to keep her feet from being crushed and her ribs from being cracked. Other couples quickly cleared out of the way to avoid being run over by the wildly twirling pair.

Fear and embarrassment encompassed Mary. She was powerless to escape Tyrone's abusive clutches. A lamb before a wolf.

The fiddlers kept playing though Cat Eye began to lose the cadence in his call. A hush fell over the spectators.

Suddenly a hand grasped Tyrone by the shoulder.

"Whoa, there son," Larry said. "Why don't we give the little lady a break."

Tyrone flung Mary aside as he viciously turned on the intruder.

"Who do you think you are?" he bellowed.

Saliva spewed as he stumbled sideways but raised his closed fists.

Mary jumped as a hand suddenly tugged at her elbow. Spinning around, she saw Susan and Les.

"Come on," urged Susan. "We gotta go."

With Les leading the way, the three pushed through the gawking crowd, transfixed by the confrontation playing out on the dance floor. As they fled into the waiting gloom, Lex plucked a lantern from a nearby light post.

"What about Larry?" called Mary.

"Larry can take care of himself," said Les. "When Susan told us what was going on, it was Larry's idea to distract Tyrone while we got you away."

"But Tyrone can be awful mean," Mary warned.

"Yeah, we know all about Tyrone Beckett," Les said. "His cousins, Garry and Trey too."

Suddenly lookin' a bit uneasy, Les snatched the hat from his head. "Beggin' your pardon, Miss Susan," he said. "I know they're your kinfolk and all."

"No need to be apologizin' to me," Susan said. "I know what folks think of them three ruffians. Makes me sad to call myself a Beckett sometimes."

A horse stamped its foot and whinnied as they hurried past his nose in the dark.

Les grinned. "Larry'll be fine," he said. "He can be mighty tough himself when need be."

They soon reached Tyrone's buggy. Les

unfastened the ground anchor and tossed it in the floorboard. He then helped the girls climb aboard before running around to the driver's side. Scrambling up, he took a seat, untied the reins, and released the brake.

"I'll get ya through the swine fields," he said. "They can be a bit tricky in the fog at night. After that, seein's how there's gonna be a full moon tonight, I reckon you'll do just fine."

Les flicked the reins and the blood bay put her weight into the harness.

"Y'all could wait on the ridge for the rest of your party, but if Tyrone and his cousins try to follow on horseback, it may not be safe."

Mary clasped Susan's hand. She hadn't thought of that.

"Course, I'll stop em if I can."

With a slight wind in their faces, they descended into the rank lowlands. The thick, swirling fog made it impossible to see the roadway. Not having taken time to light the carriage lamps, the lone lantern Les had grabbed was inadequate for the job. The buggy jostled as it ran over several fieldstones. Les reined the mare a bit to the left and their ride smoothed out.

"If we can delay them long enough, who knows?" he said. "Maybe they'll decide it's not worth the effort and just crawl off somewhere to sleep it off."

Mary and Susan both knew Tyrone's pride wouldn't let that happen. He'd not only been made to look the fool on the dance floor, but he'd lost his pa's brand-new buggy and mare to boot.

The heavy mist that had been swirling about them slowly receded as they climbed the hill beyond the swine fields. Coming to a level patch, Les reined back and murmured, "Whoa, girl."

The mare stopped and Les set the brake. Handing the reins to Mary, he climbed down and stood beside the rig.

"Want I should light the lamps for ya?"

Mary considered Tyrone seeing the light in the dark. "I don't think so," she said.

He nodded his head in understanding. "I reckon you'll be fine from here," he said. "I sure wish ya all the best of luck." He then looked at Susan. "I enjoyed our dance."

Susan beamed. "So did I," she said.

"Tell Larry we're mighty grateful," Mary said.

"I'll do that," said Les. "Now I reckon you girls better skedaddle." He took a step back. "Time's a wastin'. Be careful."

Mary thanked him and released the brake. "Bye," she and Susan both called out. She flicked the reins. The mare snickered and began plodding up the trail.

"We'll never forget your kindness," Susan yelled.

Les stood watching the buggy clatter away until it faded from sight. He then turned back toward the Colby-Hannessy farm and the ruckus that surely awaited.

This has been a day to remember, he thought with a smile. He began whistling an old ditty as he sauntered back into the fog. Only a crusty ol' bristle-haired sow and her hungry piglets laid witness to the yellow lantern's glow as it gaily swung along like a fairy-light dancing in the night.

"They were sure some fine fellas," Susan said as she scooted over and took Mary's arm in her own. The lowland mists had caused a chill that didn't seem to be letting up.

Mary felt a twinge of guilt as she pictured me and

Second Chance sittin' at home, wondering what our gals were doin'. But, after a moment, she smiled anyway.

"Yes, they were," she said.

Just as Les had predicted, not more than fifteen minutes or so, after they'd topped the ridge, a full moon filtering through the treetops. Mary's Pa had told her Mr. Colby chose that particular night for his hoe-down for just that reason; so the moon would help light the path as folks made their way home.

How he could possibly have known when the moon would be full was beyond Mary, but she was thankful it was.

While the vast forests on either side of the trail were dark and menacing, the roadway itself was bathed in soft moonlight. Nothing could stop them now.

Twenty-five minutes later she realized just how wrong that thought had been. Pulling back on the reins, she brought the buggy to a dead halt.

Ahead laid a split in the road. A perfect 'Y'. She had no idea which way to go.

"What do we do?" asked Susan.

"I don't know," said Mary. She desperately tried to remember passing the split on the way from the Cove. She and Susan had been so busy yammering they hadn't noticed it.

Now, in the dark, they hadn't a clue.

Crickets chirped ... fireflies flashed. The cacophony of nocturnal sights and sounds did nothing but add to the girls' confusion. A gentle breeze playing in the limbs of a thousand sprawling hardwoods sent a shower of multi-colored leaves drifting to the surface of the trail below. An undisturbed carpet of autumn foliage masked the junction, leaving no sign of resent travel. The forest was indifferent ... uncaring ... unconcerned.

If only they'd paid more attention, Mary brooded. *How hard would it have been to be aware of their surroundings?*

"Go right," said Susan.

"Are you sure?" Mary chirped. Perhaps Susan had been more cognizant than she'd appeared. A glimmer of hope sparked in Mary's heart.

"No, go left," Susan retracted.

"Terrific!" said Mary, deflated. "A lot of help you

are."

What to do? Suddenly, the thought of Tyrone approaching from behind spurred her into action. Either way was better than staying there.

With a flick of the reins and a click of her tongue, she urged the mare onward. They took the trail to the right.

As the buggy jostled into the recesses of the night, leaves kicked up, fluttered about, and resettled. The forest carpet remained unblemished.

Clouds gathered. The moonlight dimmed. A soft rain began to fall.

EIGHT

The Gathering Storm

THAT EVENING AFTER SUPPER, to Ma's surprise, and with Pa's approval, I rushed out to finish my chores. I was in a hurry cause I had me a mighty hankerin' to go visit with Diver. I was plumb edgy that evening, what with Mary bein' out with Tyrone, and I knew Diver always had a way of puttin' me at ease.

After I finished up, I saddled Joleen, hollered in the door I was goin' for a ride, and went to visitin'.

I can't fathom how Charlotte and Diver knew I was comin', but before I even got to the porch, Diver opened the front door and hollered out, "Come on in. Got ya a bowl of apple fritters in sweet cream sittin' on the table."

I'd never dream of lettin' on to Ma about it, but

118

not even she could make apple fritters and cream the way Charlotte did. It just somehow soothed the soul. Kinda like nestlin' in deep down under a thick warm blanket in the middle of a big ol' feather mattress while autumn rain pitter-pattered on the roof above. Made the whole world and all its woes just kinda fade away for a bit. I reckon they must have been from an ol' guarded Kentucky recipe.

As we ate, I told them Pa's story 'bout Rolf's granddaddy, the Hessian named Tobias. Diver said it didn't surprise him a lick that such a fine fellow came from noble stock.

Charlotte then excitedly pulled out a letter she'd received just that day statin' that her folks were comin' in from Kentucky to visit their new grandbaby. It said that Uncle Clive claimed to know the way and said he'd be proud to ferry 'em on down. Said he'd been hankerin' to see his Cove friends for quite a spell anyway.

Well, now I'll tell ya, that caught my attention right off. I had to chuckle. "Ma'll be frettin' over how she's gonna manage to keep her kitchen clean if that burly, bulk of a man comes up the hill a visitin'."

Course, truth be told, we all knew she'd taken quiet a shine to the gruff, but kind-hearted giant, and reckoned she'd muddle through what was to come just fine.

"Just gonna have to accept the fact that she'll be doin' a good house scubbin' when he goes home," chuckled Charlotte. "Course, so will I," she lamented.

By the time we finished with the good news 'bout Charlotte's folks comin', it was gettin' dark. Diver lit a lantern hangin' from a rafter above the game table they kept out on the porch (a spot Charlotte called her "open air visitin' parlor") and we settled in for some checkers.

The evening air was gettin' a bit crisp by then, so Charlotte slipped a soft, woolen nightgown over Pauline's dayshift and placed her in a reed basket on top of her favorite baby blanket.

Now, if you're thinkin' because Diver was my friend and mentor, he'd take it easy on me when we played a game . . . well, you'd be sorely mistaken. Diver was of a mind that you don't learn nothin' without takin' a few knocks along the way. It's them knocks that you'll remember and take to mind.

He once told me 'bout a fella that never had a want in his entire childhood. Bein' born to an older couple who feared they'd never have children, when he came along, they loved him beyond anything else in their lives. They didn't have much themselves, but if he took a fancy to something, they saw to it that he got it, no matter what. They never once let him feel disappointment. Problem was, having never done for himself, when the old couple passed during a cholera outbreak, he didn't know *how* to do for himself.

"It was a plumb shame," Diver said, "the trials and tribulations that man went through trying to adjust to life. He was nearly doomed by love and good intentions from his own adoring, but short-sighted folks. It would have been better to let him stumble now and again. It's the only way to learn to walk."

Well, when it came to checkers, Diver let me tumble plumb down the mountainside tryin' to figure out his strategy. I suppose he'd say it was heart-felt adoration and warmest intentions that led him to thumpin' me the way he done. But to my way a thinkin'; him bein' my friend and pastor and all, he sure took an unnecessary lot of pleasure outta the teachin'. I was afraid he might hurt himself just tryin' to hold in the chuckles.

After takin' two straight losses in a best out of three challenge, I sat back and happily began playin' with Pauline as Charlotte took my place at the board. To my surprise, and I must admit my amusement, it wasn't long before Charlotte began unmercifully showin' Diver how the game was played.

The chortling was suddenly comin' from the other side of the table.

For bein' such a sweet lady, Charlotte sure had a mighty competitive nature about her. She showed the man no quarter. Course, truth be told, I could see that Diver didn't really mind at all. He was 'bout swolled up with pride that Charlotte was havin' such a good time and showin' what a quick mind she had to boot.

As I sat playin' peek-a-boo with Pauline, endlessly pretending to be startled each time I whipped my hands from before my hidden eyes, it never failed to elicit a giggle from her beaming face. Fact is, I was beginnin' to think I was gonna wear out long before she did.

Then she sneezed.

"Well, bless you little one," I said.

Pauline looked startled as if wondering what had just happened.

I reached down and gently tapped the tip of her nose with my finger.

Charlotte had one of Diver's last two pieces trapped and forced the other into a losing jump.

"One more game," he said as he brushed the pine pieces back to Charlotte's side of the board.

She laughed and said, "You're a glutton for punishment."

She gathered up the stacks of black walnut pieces on her side of the table and handed them back to him. Neither of them mentioned that he had not crowned a king in that entire game.

I lowered my face close to Pauline's and tickled her ribs as I puffed out my cheeks.

She exploded with gargled laughter and flailed at my cheeks and lips with her pudgy fingers.

"You got me," I said as I kissed her on the forehead.

She sneezed again.

Charlotte and Diver stopped arranging pieces and

both looked our way.

"It's getting cold out here," Charlotte said as she pushed back her chair to retrieve Pauline.

Diver stood up and opened the front door.

"I'll stoke up the fire," he said. "Let's finish playing inside."

It was then that I felt a gentle gust of cool air tickle the short hairs on the back of my neck. It *was* getting colder. Walkin' to the far railing of the porch, I briskly rubbed my hands together and looked up toward Rich Mountain. The clear night sky was darkening as if a storm was rollin' in. The mountain tops dimmed, then slowly faded to black. A far-off discharge rippled across the sky, silently illuminating the thickening clouds. I could smell the approaching rain.

I figured the folks at the hoedown should be on their way home by then. It was gonna be a long cold ride. At least Tyrone's buggy had a top. That should help. Those in open wagons weren't gonna be so lucky. Hopefully, everyone had brought plenty of blankets to ward off the cool night air.

Hurryin' back to the door, I told Charlotte and

Diver a storm was blowin' in, so I'd better be headin' back up the hill.

They thanked me for comin' and Charlotte gave me the remainin' apple fritters to take along. It just so happened that Pa loved Charlotte's fritters even more then I did. I figured, with a little luck, one or two might survived the trek home.

"I think we're goin' the wrong way," cried Susan for what must have been the umpteenth time. She violently pulled her blanket tighter around her shoulders and tucked her chin in against the cold.

As the rain increased, the winds picked up, and the temperature dropped. Mary could see small puffs of condensation expelled from the sodden mare's nostrils as she gamely trotted along. Sinister black clouds slowly rolled in over the mountain, drawing a veil of darkness across the heavens. One by one the twinkling celestial lights were extinguished. The harvest moon and the far-off planets disappeared. The seemingly endless multitude of nocturnal insects ceased their calling and retreated to unseen refuges beneath fallen leaves or loose-fittin' bark.

"I told you to go left, but you went right," Susan lamented.

The buggy shuttered as a front wheel dropped into yet another rain filled rut in the rocky trail.

Susan "eeked" and grabbed her armrest.

"I don't know why you went right. You never listen to what I say. Now we're stuck out here in the dark and we're goin' the wrong way. I *don't want* to go this way. I want to go home. Why don't we turn around?"

Mary bit her tongue. She knew Susan tended to ramble when she was nervous, but things were far too hectic at the moment to kowtow to her fears. If she'd stop her whining for a minute, she might realize Mary wanted to go home too. Fact is, between the narrow trail and the quickly worsening weather, there was simply no way *to* turn around. What, with the skittish blood mare bolting at every peal of thunder and flash of lightening, it was all she could do just to keep the buggy on the two track.

A half an hour had passed since they'd left the 'Y'. Half an hour of spine-chilling switchbacks, bone-jarring washboards, and long descents down deeply eroded, rain-slick mountainsides.

And all the while, the rain intensified.

Not once had they found a spot level enough to stop the rig—much less to turn it back.

What did Susan want from her? she thought. *She should be happy they were still on four wheels.*

As they neared the bottom of a long, steep decline, pushin' through a tangled mass of sagging, rain-soaked rhododendrons, they suddenly came to an impasse. A swollen stream of muddy water gushed across the roadway before tumbling off the precipice on the downhill side.

Fightin' back against the weight of the buggy, the mare locked her front knees and desperately dug her hooves into the hardpack beneath her. Mary jammed her feet on the dashboard and wrenched the brake handle. Forward momentum slowed but didn't stop. The decline was too steep. The roadway and wheels too slick.

The rig shuddered and creaked as it inched forward.

Being forcefully pushed into the torrent, the horse

127

snickered and whinnied and strained with all her might. Her eyes bulged and her ears laid flat. Great billows of hot air blasted from her heaving lungs. A hoof slipped. Then another. Nothing she did could hold back the driving weight behind her. With a sudden squeal of terror, she leaped forward, trying to hurdle the cascade.

Mary released the brake and grasped the rein rail for dear life. The buggy shot into the deluge.

Muddy water slammed into the carriage spokes and underbelly. Soggy debris splattered Susan's cheek and soaked her blanket. A long-dead section of twisted dogwood ripped the passenger carriage lamp from its pinning's then washed under the floorboards, banging, and scraping as it went. The buggy tilted. In moments, the deluge would force them over the abyss.

Out of desperation, Mary scrambled across the seat and climbed on top of Susan adding her weight to the high side of the vehicle. With a clap of iron rims on water-soaked bedrock, the buggy slammed down but continued its sideways sweep. The rear wheels had lost purchase. The current was too strong.

A shudder vibrated through the carriage. Doom

was inevitable.

Suddenly, the mare reared and screamed. Terror seized her. Her muscles bunched and strained with a power she had never known before. Her mighty chest slammed into the thick harness. The sturdy calks Hec Rucker had forged into her iron shoes found purchase in the natural cracks of the bedrock. With an all-consuming bid for self-preservation, she blindly drove ahead. The cumbersome buggy shot from the raging torrent.

Even Orwell's Mammoth Jack would have been hard pressed to accomplish such a feat.

As the rig clattered from the cascade, wildly flinging muck in its wake, a dreadful rumble billowed from the hillside above. The ground quaked. The surrounding vegetation quivered. The crescendo intensified as if the mountain itself had collapsed from the onslaught of the storm. It swiftly drew near.

Susan screamed.

The mare shrieked and doubled her efforts.

Mary clasped her hands tight on the rein rail.

Seconds passed before a great torrent of rocks, mud, and fallen timber, swept down the narrow gully, obliterating the landscape mere inches behind the retreating rear wheels of the buggy. A deafening crash rent the night as the deadly mass slammed into the low water ford they had so recently escaped. What had moments before been their route home, was now a solid wall of boulders, saturated soil, and splintered wood.

The pass was gone.

Quickly surmounting the top of the incline, Mary reined back on the frightened horse and set the brake. The mare whinnied and stomped. Her withers quivered. Yet she obeyed and stood in place.

Thunder rumbled in the swollen clouds above.

Mary sat stunned and shivering in the dark. Cold rain streamed in unnoticed rivulets down her hair and face, soaking into her dress. The same dress she had so proudly sashayed before me when thrilled about goin' to the dance. It was now a tangled, misshapen mass of soggy material. Even her pretty sunhat and ribbon had somehow disappeared along the way.

Shaking uncontrollably, she sat gasping for air, trying hard not to cry. In the pouring rain it would have been impossible to tell if she was succeeding.

Lookin' to her right, she saw a blanket wrapped, quivering heap, curled up on the floorboard. A long, drawn-out whimper, interrupted occasionally by hic-up like snorts, emanated into the night.

"We . . . we . . . we're safe," Mary said.

"Eeee" was the only reply she received. Not a particularly helpful discourse, but knowing Susan, the best she could expect for quite some time.

As Mary sat back on the cushioned buggy seat letting her heart rate settle, she wondered what to do next. The night was abysmal, she was exhausted, and without bein' able to retrace their tracks, they were truly lost. Before she'd set out with Tyrone earlier that day, the only exposure she'd had to the wilderness was travelin' to and from the Cove with her father or takin' our short forages to the apple orchard. She imagined Susan knew even less.

With the shock of the harrowing stream crossing and landslide wearin' off, an awareness of the frigid air began to settle in. She shivered and wrapped her arms around herself; briskly rubbing her shoulders in a failed attempt at warmth. Where was her blanket?

Leaning forward, she blindly felt around on the

rain-soaked floorboard and under the seat.

No luck.

Sitting back up, she twisted around and reached over the lazy-back. The buggy was designed with a small, boxed-in storage compartment behind the seat that could accommodate a few light packages or often needed supplies.

Desperately flailing about in the dark with quickly numbing fingers, her heart sank as the trunk revealed nothin' more than the floorboard had.

"No," she moaned.

Her stomach painfully clinched in despair.

Just then lightning rippled across the sky.

To Mary's amazement, it lit a dangling flap of muddy material wrapped tightly around the buggy's axil. The blanket! How it had become lodged between the undercarriage and the iron hub of the wheel was beyond her, but there it was.

Thrilled with the discovery, she happily leaped from the buggy, slipped in the muck, missed at an attempt to grab a wooden spoke, and landed in a rain-pelted puddle on her backside.

"Ugh!" she groaned.

Sittin' on the ground with legs splayed, and wet, tangled hair draped across her face, she slapped the murky water like a baby in the throes of a tantrum.

Susan wasn't the only one who could show a temper.

After a moment to calm down, and with the bone-numbing cold prompting her to get up, she sloshed over to the carriage and untangled the blanket.

It being wool, she knew it would retain heat, wet or dry. As for the mud? Well, there wasn't a thing it could do to her tattered, filthy, rain-soaked party dress that hadn't already been done.

Climbin' back into the buggy, Mary quickly wrung out the blanket the best she could under the semi-protection of the oil treated leather roof. She then ground her teeth and shivered as she wrapped the wet material around her shoulders. Minutes passed before her body heat started collecting among the fibers.

"You might want to sit up," she called to Susan. "We're about to get under way."

"No!" snapped Susan, pullin' her blanket tighter. She remained on the floor.

Okay, thought Mary as she gathered up the reins

and released the brake, *have it your way*.

With a flick of the wrist, they began clamoring down the trail — jostlin' and jarrin' as they went. Within moments Susan climbed into her seat. Staring at the dark, neither girl mentioned the small goose egg startin' to rise on her forehead.

The rain eased a bit but continued to fall. The buggy jostled along through the stygian night. The trail grew ever narrower and more overgrown. Weeds and brush soon obscured the pathway. Only a gap between the trees gave testament to the way forward. Before long Mary gave the mare her head. She was better equipped to traverse the dark anyway.

As the witching hour drew near, the girls gave in to exhaustion and fell into a troubled asleep.

NINE

Dilemma

CRACK! THE FRONT LEFT corner of the buggy slammed to the ground. Mary was flung forward. If not for her legs gettin' tangled in the wrought iron bench supports, she would have been thrust over the low dashboard and trampled beneath the hooves of the startled mare. Oddly enough, she was rudely awakened with Susan Beckett's impressive weight crashing down on her skinned and bruised calf muscles.

Pain racked her shins as the terrified girl instantly went into a blind frenzy, having no idea how she had come to be tangled, face down, among the cold, damp, folds of Mary's long hem. Only half awake and totally disoriented, she screamed and kicked and struck out like an infant in a fit.

"Settle down!" Mary shouted, trying to grab Susan's flailing hands without taking a blow to the face. "Let me help you up."

After finally gettin' pulled into an upright position; sittin' on the badly sloping seat next to Mary, Susan sat shocked and bewildered as she stared into the menacing, unfamiliar wilderness about them. Her eyes were wide and disbelieving as she asked, "What happened. Where are we?"

"I don't know," said Mary. She looked down at the left front wheel lyin' shattered on the rock-strewn ground. The iron-clad felloes and several wooden spokes laid tangled among a scattering of heavy granite boulders. A section of splintered axel still protruded from the hub.

"We seem to have broken that thing that holds the wheel on," she said.

"Can you fix it?" asked Susan.

Mary sat dumbstruck.

"Can I fix it?" she blurted. "How am I supposed to fix it?"

Ripping a jagged, foot-long swathe of material from her clingin' dress as she climbed down from the carriage, she stood lookin' at the damage and said, "Why don't *you* fix it?"

Susan followed Mary to the ground. Tears welled in her eyes.

"We're never gonna get home," she wept.

Mary wrapped her arms around the terrified girl and hugged her. She previously thought she knew everything there was to know about the spunky little firecracker. But in all truth, does anybody really know anyone else. Never had she imagined that Susan could be so frightened and vulnerable. That she could let slip the tough veneer she so emphatically clung to and show the frightened child that dwelled within.

Seein' her friend's frailty only strengthened Mary's resolve. The very tribulations that might have easily tilted the scales and dragged her into the depths of despair, somehow had the opposite effect. She knew, for the sake of them both, she had to be strong.

"Sure, we will," she said, trying hard to quail her own fears. "Why, we'll be home in no time, wrapped in warm blankets, laughing about the great adventure we had. Just you wait and see"

As she talked, the yellow-orange glow of daybreak

began to filter through the tall, straight, tree trunks. An unexpected display that somehow seemed surreal in the midst of their agonies.

It looks just like a big ol' shelf of chicken of the woods mushrooms, she thought.

The brilliant colors filled her eyes and calmed her spirit. She stood transfixed in the glow. For a fleeting moment, she was at peace. How could one not take heart in the face of such beauty?

Then, as if to stifle any inkling of burgeoning hope, the gently falling rain intensified with the dawning, and muted the effect to greyness. A wall of liquid despair reestablished its grip over the woodlands. A rumble of far-off thunder rolled through the lonely hollows.

Nature is the great diplomat. It looks on with indifference and disregard to both the longevity of the mighty mountains and the fleeting existence of the delicate flowers. It professes to be neither ally nor nemesis to the noblest of kings or the lowest of beasts. It stands unmoved and aloof in the face of hard-won victories or crushing defeats endured in the mortal struggle. For one in need, it may be either the giver of shelter and sustenance, or the harbinger of death. The allotment of each, metered out in equal measure.

Yet, deep in Mary's heart burned an ember of hope. A truth she had known from her earliest days. The pivotal theme of her father's every sermon, and every axiom. The unwavering belief in the eternal love of God. She took just a moment to close her eyes and recite the most powerful prayer ever uttered.

Thy will be done.

With the surrounding forest cocooned in a steady din of falling rain, daybreak advanced across the sky pushing a gentle breeze before it.

Mary shivered.

We need to find somewhere to get out of this rain for a while," she told Susan.

Workin' together, the girls stripped the mare from her trace and harness, freein' her from the restraints of the buggy. Then they shortened the reins by weaving them back and forth through the cheekpieces of the bit. Not having a saddle and stirrups to help them get on the horse, they led her around to stand on the high side of the buggy. Each girl, stifling her fear of sliding off the towering beast, draped her blanket over her head and clasped it tight as she clambered up the tilted seat and climbed aboard.

Susan squealed . . . Mary groaned . . . and the blood bay mare flicked her tail and snorted as if she was annoyed with the whole affair.

It may have been better than walkin' through the mire, but sittin' on cold, clammy, bristle-haired, horsehide with bare, goose bump mottled legs, didn't lend much credence to a girl feelin' ladylike. That, along with cold, wet, stringy locks plastered to their face and shoulders like last night's leftover pasta was about more than any young woman could stand.

"I'm never chaperonin' for you again," said Susan.

"Well, who asked ya?" returned Mary.

After a moment to think about it, she said, "If ya gotta blame somebody, blame your brother."

"Ooh," Susan hissed as she nashed her teeth. "When I get ahold of him!"

Mary couldn't help but grin. If she wasn't so furious with Tyrone, she'd almost feel sorry for him. When they got back. (If they got back.) He had a reckonin' a comin'.

Well, at least Susan had said, 'When I get ahold

of him', thought Mary. *She must be more confident we'll get out of this than she had been letting on.*

"That's if we don't die out here in the wilderness," Susan grumbled.

And then again, maybe not, thought Mary.

Urging the horse along, unaware of where they were or which way to go, they only knew they weren't where they wanted to be. As the morning waned, and the chilly rains came and went, they passed through a forest of towering trees. Ridge after ridge, hollow after hollow, disappointment mounted as each hopeful glimpse from high mountain passes revealed nothing more than endless peaks and far-reaching woodlands. Not a single hint of human presence had been evident since they lost the roadway somewhere before the buggy had been shattered.

Surely, no wayward traveler or ramblin' outcast had ever trodden these lonely, misty, hills.

By what Mary guessed to be noon (It was hard to tell with the skies being as hazy as they were.) they stopped at the mouth of a long valley. Lookin' off into the distance, they could see a wide pool of murky water bordered by overgrown marshlands. The pond looked as though it covered the floor of the hollow from wall to wall.

"Looks like we'll have to turn back and go around," said Mary.

"Go around how?" blurted Susan. "What difference does it make which way we go?"

"Well, we know what's behind us," said Mary. "Nothin' but endless forest and an unpassable mudslide." She tucked her lank hair behind her ears for the millionth time. "So, we may as well see what's in front of us."

They sat for a moment in silence. Each in her own thoughts; scared, tired, cold and confused about how they had wound up in the predicament they were in. Even though the rain had stopped a quarter hour before, neither had noticed.

"Of course, if you have a better idea," quipped Mary, "feel free to share."

Susan sat shaking her head. She used the lacey cuff of her party dress to wipe her nose. Something she would have been appalled at if she'd seen anyone else do it.

"I'm hungry, and thirsty, and cold," she said.

Mary held her tongue. So was she. She couldn't fault the girl on that account.

Layin' the reins alongside the blood bay's neck and gently pullin' to the left, the horse started to turn. Just then a slight breeze played across the quagmire, dividin' the mist. A shadowy form was glimpsed far off in the distance.

"Whoa," said Mary. "What was that?"

"What was what?" asked Susan.

"I thought I saw somethin' on the far side of the valley," said Mary. She pointed toward the spot of the vestige. "Over there," she said.

"I don't see anything," said Susan.

"Just wait and watch," urged Mary.

Minutes passed as they strained to make out what Mary had seen. A thick haze hung over the valley. Drizzling rain drifted across the glade. Mary began to doubt her own senses. Perhaps it had been nothing. After all, it *had* been a long morning.

Then, a stout breeze swept down the ridge.

The mist swirled. The rain eased. The haze faded and then parted like a delicate curtain drawn back by giant hands.

"I see it!" shouted Susan as she beat Mary on the back with one hand and pointed with the other. "I see it! It's a cabin!"

Mary squinted as she studied the structure. It was a small, probably one room shanty, sitting on a wedge of raised land, well back in the tree line. No smoke, animals or activity of any kind gave indication that it was inhabited.

"Probably a trapper's cabin," said Mary. "Maybe he can help us. Let's find a way around this field."

Following the base of the ridge they soon found a game trail. It seemed the wild critters of the forest were no more inclined to traverse the quagmire than the girls were. In their minds were visions of a warm fire, dry clothes, and perhaps even a hot meal. Their ordeal was nearly over.

Unfortunately, the closer they came to the miraculous, wilderness sanctuary, the more their hearts sank. The moss-covered walls were sagging and would probably have collapsed years ago if not for the massive growth of Virginia Creepers clinging to the logs. The single window contained nothing more than a narrow, foot-long strip of brown, moldy, oilcloth that creaked like a flap of birchbark in the cool breeze. Where the door had once stood was now a gaping hole in the wall that exuded the foul stench of deep-set rot and crumbling wood-decay. Worst of all, and what they couldn't have possibly seen at a distance through the low-hanging foliage, was the roof. There wasn't one.

As if to add insult to injury, a low-hanging cloud filled the sky, and a cold rain began falling once again.

Reaching back, Mary took Susan's arm.

"Let me help you down," she said. "We have to find shelter."

Susan was so tired and disappointed she didn't even have the energy to complain. Taking Mary's hand, she simply slid to the ground and stood there, shivering in ankle deep mud.

Mary then flopped over on her stomach and dropped to the ground next to Susan. And stuck!

As she teetered, flailing her arms, and grasping for help, Susan just stood and watched. If not for a small sapling nearby, she would have landed face down in the mud.

"Thanks a lot," she said to Susan.

Susan made no comment. Her face was blank.

Tying the horse's reins to the sapling, Mary grasped Susan's arm and led her toward the shack. As they slogged through the mud, lightning rippled across the cloud laden sky. The delicate hairs on Mary's arms seemed to prickle and stand on end with the discharge. Thunder rumbled as it rolled across the valley. Whatever reprieve they had been given, had apparently come to an end.

Mary grimaced as a pang of protest clinched her innards. Both girls had drank as much rainwater as possible, (often by squeezing it from their blankets) but food was sorely lacking. Over the last hour or so their stomachs had taken to grumblin' just about as much as the skies above.

Arriving at the open doorway, it soon became evident what had caused most of the damage to the cabin. A massive cottonwood tree had been uprooted in some long-ago storm and crashed down through the roof. The interior was now a shattered tangle of sticks and twigs, along with a splintered section of shake shingle roof that had come to rest at an angle along the rear wall.

From her vantage point, Mary could make out a two-foot gap at one end of it that might give access to the space below. Assuming there was a space below.

"If there's room under that roof that isn't full of debris, it just might make a good temporary shelter," Mary said.

Susan pulled her blanket tighter around her shoulders and didn't reply.

"Could get us out of this rain," Mary continued.

Still nothing from Susan.

Exasperated, Mary wanted nothing more than to reach out and shake the girl. Get some kind of a reaction out of her. Instead, she bit her tongue and let it be. What good would it do?

Wiping the rain from her eyes, she said, "You stand here and guard the door. I'll go in and check it out."

Susan nodded.

Great, thought Mary. *Now she responds.*

Struggling through mounds of shattered debris — slimy, moldy, and foul-smelling, from years of encroaching vegetation, Mary gradually made her way to the opening. Every few feet she had to stop and untangle her tattered dress from a splintered limb or scrape a revolting clump of decomposition from her hands or face. As much as possible, she cleared a path as she went, in hopes of avoiding some of the muck on the way out. The stench was nearly beyond comprehension.

Finally reaching the gap, she knelt down and hesitantly eased her head into the dark confines.

The space smelled of dirt, wood rot, and something similar to wet dogs. The only sounds were the pattering of rain on weathered shakes and a dangling piece of gnarled limb that insistently scraped back and forth on the roof like an out-of-time metronome.

Crawling in out of the rain, she placed her back against the wall and hugged her knees as she waited for her eyes to adjust. The feel of dry dirt beneath her was more luxurious than any feather mattress she had ever lain on. It seemed weeks since she'd been in out of the rain.

Was the dance really just yesterday?

It would be so easy to close her eyes and drift away into wonderful sleep, letting Susan stand out there in the monsoon by herself all day if that's what she chose to do. Of course, Mary knew she could never do such a thing. As exasperating as the girl could be sometimes, she was still Mary's closest friend.

Openin' her heavy eyes, she looked down the tunnel-like space. Amazed, she realized she could make out the dim interior after all. Numerous clods of chinking in the log walls had crumbled over time allowin' dingy beams of muted light to filter through the dark. A welcoming, though ghostly pallor, hung over the semidarkness.

Gettin' on her hands and knees, Mary flung her blanket as far as she could, and slowly began to crawl down the eight-foot passage after it. Not an easy task in a long dress. For every shuffle forward she first had to cast her hem before her. If not, the material would clamp down tight on her neck and nearly choke her. After advancing a couple feet, she'd have to fling the blanket once again and repeat the whole process. It was slow and frustrating. *Boys must have it so much easier in trousers*, she thought. But at least there was surprisingly little in the way. As if the passage had been cleared out by someone; or something.

At the end of the tunnel, tucked into the far corner of the cabin, was a wallow-like depression perhaps two-feet deep, and four-feet long. The animal smell was stronger there. A section of the hollow undermined the cabin wall by a few feet but looked dry and cozy.

In their present situation, it was about the best shelter they could hope to find, in Mary's opinion.

Droppin' her blanket into the hole, Mary got turned around and made her way back outside. Leaving the dry confines of the sloped roof was about the hardest thing she'd ever done, but she knew there was no helping it. She had to get Susan.

"Susan!" Mary shouted as she shook the girl, calling her name for the third time.

Susan finally came back from wherever she'd been in her mind and looked at Mary.

Truth is, she looked more like a half-drowned possum than the cute, spunky, girl that had been flirting with the boys at the hoe-down the night before.

"Susan," Mary said again, focusing on the girl's

150

eyes. "Get in under the roof. It's a bit smelly, but it's dry. We can stay there until the rain stops."

She turned the girl and gave her a slight push, getting her started on her way.

"I'll be right there. I have to check on the horse."

Watching Susan for a moment to make sure she was going to do what she was told, Mary then hurried over to the mare.

"How ya doin' girl?" Mary crooned.

The horse blew and nibbled at Mary's wet collar.

"You don't want that," Mary said, pushin' the long snout away from her neck. "But I can fix you up with something better."

In her hurry when they arrived, Mary had tied the reins too short for the mare to reach the thick grasses and water filled puddles in the clearing. Now, workin' with numb fingers, she unwound everything from the horse's cheekpieces and retied the much longer tether to the sapling. The leather reins were swollen with water, but she hoped they'd hold.

"That oughta take care of ya," said Mary.

The horse immediately went to munching the damp greenery. It apparently felt no thanks was warranted as it swished its tail and turned its rump to the chill breeze.

Turnin', to head back to the shelter, something caught Mary's eye.

Rhubarb? What's rhubarb doing here?

She hurried over to pluck the red stalk. Nearby grew three more. And green onions. She even found a half dozen turnup greens.

The old trapper who had lived there must have planted a vegetable garden long ago to supplement his table fare. When he departed its perennial offerings continued to flourish. Each spring and summer they returned. Each fall they went to seed. The following year they repeated the process. It was as if they were waiting for Mary and Susan. Waiting until they were needed the most.

Gathering up her bounty, Mary hurried to show Susan what she'd found. If anything was going to revive the girl, this would do it.

Crawling down the dark passage, Mary couldn't help but grin. This was gonna to be better than Christmas.

Suddenly, she stopped.

"OH, NO YOU DON'T!" she cried as she dropped the veggies.

Susan was in the depression, curled up tight in *both* their blankets, snoring away.

Mary dove in the hole on top of her.

"Give it to me!" she roared as she pulled on her blanket.

A suddenly awakened and not at all happy Susan growled, "No, it's mine."

"Not both of them ain't." claimed Mary.

The struggle was loud and fierce, but as weary as both girls were ... short lived. Finally, each wrapped in her own blanket, they sat quietly chewing on hard, cold vegetables. Mary felt she'd be fortunate if she didn't lose a tooth.

Within fifteen minutes they were both sound asleep — wet clothes and all.

TEN

Vigil

PASTOR WILSON SAT IN what he called, his "study"; a four-by-six-foot cubical he had partitioned off from his already inadequate bedroom as an area for scripture study and sermon writing. It consisted of a high-gloss, bee's wax polished, roll-top writer's desk, and a straight-back chair softened with an overstuffed, down filled cushion. On top of the desk sat a crystal whale oil lantern with a beautiful hand-painted chimney and fuel receptacle given to him and his bride by his parents as a wedding gift.

In the wall, above the desk was an eight-paned window covered with a finely woven lace curtain decorated with a Biblical scene. The curtain had taken Mary more than two months to create under the tutelage of Miss Mellencamp and was among Wilson's most cherished possessions; along with the lamp and his leather-bound Bible.

As he touched quill to paper, yet another glob of ink smudged his notations. At this rate his missive was quickly becomin' a spattering of black stains rather than a list of talking points.

If only someone could invent an affordable writing instrument with a saturation proof nib, he lamented.

After scraping excess ink from the worn-out quill back into the inkwell, and wipin' off the tip, he dropped it into a small, mottled, pinewood box alongside five other defunct feathers. He'd soon need to take the lot of 'em over to Hester Wo's cobbler shop and have him recut the tips.

Besides being a blind cobbler, Mr. Wo was a fine 'pen mender'. (A tedious job very few craftsmen could master; creatin' an edge that released the precise amount of fluid to achieve the desired line ... be it bold or fine). On top of that, he had to be able to mirror each cut to accommodate the hand of either a right or a left-handed scribe. Not an easy task for a sharp-eyed mender. How a blind man who couldn't even see the written word achieved such a feat was considered by many as nothin' shy of miraculous.

Having a quill recut, (or mended), was costly, but still far cheaper than purchasing a newly cured and cut writing instrument.

As Paster Wilson retrieved a fresh quill from the holder on top of his desk, he noticed a shadow play across the window.

Strange, he thought. He pulled his pocket watch from his vest and studied the time. Six twenty-seven.

Scootin' his chair back to rise, he unknowingly drug the base of his thumb through the ink blob, obliterating his notes. (As so often is the case, his later revision produced a better sermon anyway).

Strolling through the living room to the front door, he pulled back the curtain and looked out. The evening glow had become overcast and dreary. A cluster of fallen leaves swirled across the front yard. Gamma grass growing along his fencerow swayed in the wind.

Openin' the door, he walked out onto the porch and stood gazing at the distance. Dark clouds were gathering over the mountains. Pillows of thickening mist floated across the slate-blue sky dulling it into a sinister green hue. An early twilight was settlin' over the valley.

As silent bursts of lightning glowed among the far-off mountain peaks, a stiff breeze whipped across the pastor's well-maintained lawn and tousled his thinning hair. Absentmindedly reachin' up, he brushed it back in place. Unfortunately, the hand he used was the same one he had so recently brushed through the smudged ink on his notes.

A soot-black smear colored his hair from his cheekbone to his right ear. For all intents and purposes, it appeared as though he had attempted to darken the salt and pepper locks of his right temple. Also, to his dismay, when he later discovered his mishap, it was too late. The stain had set. There was nothin' for it but to let his hair grow out enough to cut away the blotch.

I can tell ya true, until that follicle feat had been accomplished, not a few of the church ladies tsked their tongues each Sunday morning at the sight of him. After all, it hadn't been but a fortnight since he caused a row among the ladies by deliverin' a sermon

157

on pride and vanity.

And just when Delma had placed a brand-new shipment of calico print on sale too.

As Wilson watched the impending storm clouds gather, he fingered his watch one more time. Pullin' it from his vest pocket, he thumbed the crown-spring mechanism to release the engraved hunter lid. Six thirty-four. An hour and a half or so till the hoe-down was to wrap up. And from the Colby-Hannessy farms beyond the west slope of Rich Mountain, the revelers may not even be aware of the onslaught they would soon be headed into.

"Lord, watch over your children," he prayed. "Deliver them from this tempest."

Then, even as a cool breeze sent a shiver down his spine like an icy finger of doom, he pleaded, "Bring my Mary home safe."

After biddin' Charlotte and Diver farewell, I tightened Joleen's cinch strap, climbed aboard, and pointed her head for home. We hadn't cleared the B&C before darkness enveloped the skies. The stars vanished and I felt as if I was floatin' in a great cauldron of eternal night.

Fact is, it was so dark out there I don't reckon I'd be strayin' too far off the path to say I wasn't real certain when I had my eyes open, or when I had em shut. I'm tellin' ya, I couldn't see a thing. My world was cloaked in shadow.

It was quiet too. As I recall, there was nary a sound other than the steady patter of heavy droplets cascading from one over-burdened leaf to another. That, and the occasional clack of Joleen's hoofs striking cobblestones in the sodden trail now and again. It was as if all God's creatures, great and small, had slunk away into the night, tryin' to hide from the deluge they knew was comin'.

The swirling mist, as thick as 'possum chowder, only eased on occasion when tamped down by the weight of a light shower of chilly rain. Even then, when the drizzle eased, it billowed back up to obscure the world yet again.

Truth be told, it was a bit creepy bein' out there all by my lonesome.

Now, don't get me wrong. I ain't sayin' I was

afraid of the dark or nothin' like that. I just reasoned it was plumb wasteful to have a perfectly good fireplace blazin' away at home when I wasn't there to enjoy it.

I prodded Joleen into a quicker gait. She flicked her tail and snickered her annoyance but complied—for a moment. Then, after an accelerated stride or two, she settled right back into her chosen pace. I reckon she figured if she was doin' the work, she'd do it as she saw fit.

Fact is, there really wasn't a whole lot I could do about it either. Not unless I wanted to climb down and trade places with her. And that wasn't gonna happen. How demeaning would it be if Pa were to see me trudgin' up the hill with Joleen sittin' on my shoulders. Her just a snickerin' as she prodded me along tryin' to get me t' pick-up the pace?

No, he'd never let me hear the end of it.

I decided I'd just stay right where I was and put up with the ambling progress. We'd get there when we got there.

It was just about then that a blinding flash of flickering light lit-up the night. A great slash of blue-green fire ripped apart a nearby tree from crown to root base. Bark and debris rained down from the heavens like hailstones. For an instant there my eyeballs felt as if they had burst from my head as glowing orbs of brilliance obscured my vision. I didn't even have time to blink away the pain before a deep, booming thunderclap exploded over my shoulders like ol' John Paul Jones himself loosening a full-fleet cannonade against the British. The concussion of the blast slammed the air from my lungs.

It was then that Joleen decided she was anxious to get home after all. I simply held on to the saddle and went along for the ride. Turned out, that old mule could burn-a-shuck right quick when she had a mind to.

Within minutes my sight had returned to some semblance of normal, though my ears still sizzled like ten-thousand crickets had taken up residence in my noggin.

I can tell ya, I was some happy when we finally clambered out of that crypt-like trail and into the open spaces of Pa's homestead. I don't reckon there ever was a more comforting sight than comin' home

161

and seein' that yeller glow of light spillin' out across the cabin's front porch from Ma's bedroom window.

I reckon I'd o' given my eye teeth to rush on in there out of the cold and kick back for a spell. Grab a cup of Ma's hot coffee and cuddle up close to the fire.

Course, that ain't how things are done, livin' on a farm and all. There's always chores awaitin' that ain't gonna take care of themselves.

"Get them outta the way first," is what Pa taught me. "Then you can study on restin' yer weary bones for a bit."

As I rode across the yard, the front door of the cabin opened. I couldn't tell in the dark for sure who was standing there, but by the way the shadow near blocked the entire doorway, I figured it must be Pa.

I waved.

A blur of shadow indicated he must have waved back. A second later, the door closed.

I continued on across the barnyard bridge as a steady rain began to fall in earnest. It was plenty cold where it found a way past my collar and down my back side, I can tell ya. But all in all, I was mighty happy it'd waited off for the most part tell I got home.

It wasn't long before Joleen was stripped of tack and curried. She then ambled back out into the night, no doubt lookin' for the reassurances of her longtime companion, Mac.

It always did seem odd to me that none of Pa's mules ever cared much for bein' stabled out of the rain. That is at least except for on the cruelest of winter days, during the harshest of icy storms. As long as they could place their tails to the wind and hang their heads low as they napped, they were happy as a polecat in a laundry basket. Kinda made my skin all goose bumpy to think about it, is what it done. But I guess, as they say, to each his own.

After Joleen left, I looked after Tilly and her new calf; the one Ma called Nelly after Nelly Curtis Lewis: Martha Washington's granddaughter. She had only met the girl once, by chance, when they were children, but she said Nelly was the prettiest girl she'd ever seen. How that relates to naming a cow after her, I don't know. But Ma named it, so me and Pa used it.

I then proceeded to milk our newest acquisition; an Ayrshire named Dander. Yep, another one of Ma's namin's.

Now, Dander didn't come to us by way of our neighbor, Clarence Tudwell, like the rest of our livestock did. She came from a passing homesteader who was in need of corn seed for his first year's plantin'. He'd heard that Pa had the best seed in the region and was anxious to trade his three-year-old, Ayrshire cow for a sack of the golden nuggets.

I reckon the fact that his cow was naturally polled had more than a little bit to do with him lookin' to be shy of her. Most Appalachian farmers didn't cotton much to hornless livestock. Looked at 'em as homely and low-bred. Especially an Ayrshire. They normally carried a delicately curved, black-tipped spire that any man would be proud to have as his favorite powder horn. But hornless?

Be that as it may, how they figured a hornless critter, be it cow, goat, or buffalo, is somehow inferior to a horned one was a puzzle to me. What's horns got to do with milk?

Reckon Pa saw it like I did. After checkin' that gal out from stem to stern; givin' her a test milkin' and samplin' the silky libations she offered, he shook the man's hand to seal the deal.

164

Turned out that cow just may have given the sweetest milk I ever drank.

Be it hinnies, mules, or prize-winning hogs, I don't think I ever saw Pa walk away from a barter second best. Yet, in every instance, the other fella went home smilin' like he was the one who skinned the skunk.

Course, all I was meanin' to tell ya was, when Ma saw the Ayrshire, she was mighty taken with it. Said it had the prettiest red and white coat she'd ever seen on a bovine. Only thing was, both sides of its deep red neck was splattered in tiny white speckles. Looked to her like the poor thing had a bad case of dandruff.

And so, Ma named her Dander.

It didn't take long to finish the milkin'. I then wrapped up tight again, made a mad dash across the rain-slick bridge, and sloshed my way around back to deposit my bucket of fresh milk in the springhouse.

As I ran past the porch, I noticed Baby stretched out on her old tattered banket near Pa's rocker. She'd somehow managed to squiggle around enough to at least partially get herself wrapped in the rough, but warm material. As I scrambled by, her eyes followed me, but she made no move to join me in my romp-in-the-rain. Guess I can't really blame her. Probably figured if I was fool enough to wait for the sky to collapse before doin' my chores, I deserved what I got.

After all, she was doin' *her* job.

After placin' the milk in the springhouse and weightin' down the lid with a good-sized rock. (An ongoin' attempt to keep the varmints out.) I hurried to the covered breezeway that led to Ma's kitchen. There, finally out of the rain, I stomped the muck from my boots and removed my waterlogged coat and hat. Shaking them out, I entered the back door.

The rush of warm air that engulfed me felt wonderful.

"There you are," Pa said from where he sat nursing a steaming cup of hot coffee. As he blew on the brew, a translucent wisp of vapor beaded along the tips of his bushy mustache and eyebrows. I didn't figure it'd be long before Ma got to diggin' out her hair cuttin' apron and scissors. Course, when Pa got a shearin' I would too. That was just a fact of life on the Banion homestead.

As I hung my wet overgarments on a peg by the

door, I said, "Ain't fit for a temperamental tadpole out there."

"Reckon not," Pa said as he took a cautious sip of his coffee.

I could tell it was still too hot by the way he quickly sucked in his upper lip and sat the cup back down on the table. He then wiped his mustache with his sausage sized index finger and stared at the brew as if it was being deliberately obstinate.

"Hope that little gal o' yours can swim," he said.

Bells went off in every direction.

First: I'd been tryin' everything I could, not to even think about Mary Wilson bein' off on a date with Tyrone Beckett. And especially, cuddled-up with him against the cold on the long ride home. Second: I truly was concerned about her crossin' the mountains in this kind of weather. And third: No matter how hard I fought it, there wasn't a thing I could do about my ears and the back of my neck gettin' all hot and bothered whenever Pa said, "That little gal o' yours."

It was plumb frustratin' is what it was.

Ma turned my way with a twinkle in her eye. She reached up and rubbed the back of my shoulder. "You go ahead and sit down," she said, noddin' to my regular spot across from Pa. "I'll bring ya some coffee to warm ya up."

As I sat, I could see Pa's mind just a whirlin'. I knew what he was up to. He was tryin' mighty hard to come up with another zinger he figured would finish the job and plumb set my ears to burnin'. Seemed like that had become his mission in life as of late. I hate to say it, but sometimes I missed them old days when I was a kid, and he didn't seem to know I existed.

Then an idea hit me.

"Got somethin' from Charlotte," I said.

I pulled that bundle of apple fritters out o' my shirt and placed 'em on the table.

Pa's eyes got big, and in no time at all, me and him were just a dunkin' an' a munchin' and havin' a grand ol' time. Even Ma got brave enough to reach in and grab one without gettin' her fingers bit before they were all gone. But, best of all, Pa forgot about tryin' to embarrass me. Between them fritters and the nice hot brew, he had more important things on his mind.

≈

Ten sixteen.

As Wilson nervously paced, his shoe tip snagged the corner of his living room throw rug bunching the well-worn material into an untidy heap. Pausing, he reached down and pulled it flat.

Where is that girl? he thought.

Standing up, he brushed back the curtain once again and cupped his weary eyes against the cold windowpane trying in vain to make out movement along Baptist Church Rd. It was a gesture he had surely made a hundred times in the last hour.

No luck. Nothing stirred except the wind lashed streaks of unrelenting rain.

They should be here by now.

Of course, he knew he was being unreasonable. In this kind of weather, they'd be lucky to make it back by eleven. On the other hand, he figured a father sometimes has the right to be a bit unreasonable when it comes to the safety of his only child.

A flick of his pocket watch. Ten eighteen.

What's wrong with this thing? He held the

169

timepiece up to his ear and listened as the rhythmic, tick, tick, tick, bore witness to the passage of time.

Walking into the kitchen, he picked up his cup of hot tea and took a sip.

Cold?

He dumped the tepid liquid into the dry sink and reached for the fine porcelain pot sitting on the hotplate of his cast-iron pot belly stove. Pouring a fresh cup, he sat it on the table. As a small cloud formed over the brew, he replaced the pot on the stove and returned to the widow. In but a moment, the simmering beverage was forgotten and began to cool once again.

The one comforting thought that ran through Wilson's mind was, *Casey had not yet passed by either*.

What he didn't know was that a large boxelder tree had fallen across Baptist Church Rd. near the Rich Mountain access. Until it was removed in the coming days, no one would be traveling that way.

Casey, upon discovering the obstruction, had taken a detour past Forrest's property, and followed Beckett Road to the far end of Baptist Church. From that distance, on that stormy night, he could not make out the yellow glow emanating from the pastor's windows, nor could Wilson see the carriage lantern swaying in the dark.

Making a right, Casey had then accessed Abrams Creek Bridge on his way to Cades Cove Road. Neither man realized that even as Wilson's tea sat cooling on his dining table, it had been a quarter of an hour since Casey had dropped off the Tudwells and Thelma at Dean's place. He was presently in the act of wiping down Diver's carriage in the McCoy barn, before saddling up his mammoth jack and riding home.

Ten forty-two.

Wilson could stand it no longer. He had to talk to someone about the over-due hoedown caravan or he felt he was gonna burst. The most logical person to contact would be Trace Beckett. After all, surely, he must be just as concerned about his own kids being late.

Picturing the route in his mind, he decided not to bother saddling his horse. The quickest route to Trace's place would be cross country, rain or not.

He'd Follow Baptist Church Road to Lion's Den

Bluff Trail. (So named because legend claims an old trapper killed a panther in the small cave there and took her infant cub home to raise by hand. Things went well for a few months, until the juvenile cat decided to test the old platitude about bitin' the hand that feeds ya. Cotts, or Potts, was lucky he survived the infection that set into his mangled hand and shredded fingers. As for the panther, he lit a shuck, and was never seen again.)

Near the end of Lion's Den Bluff, he could follow Thom Greer's back pasture fence line to South Loop Lane, then cut across Scotsman's field to Trace Beckett's backdoor.

With luck, he should be there in fifteen minutes.

After leaving a note on the table in case Mary should arrive before he returned and wrapping up tight in all the fowl-weather gear he owned, he set out.

Twenty-seven minutes later, a half frozen, half drowned, Pastor Wilson of the Cades Cove Baptist Church stood shivering and dripping water on the hand-polished, hardwood floors in Trace and Odette Beckett's living room.

"You came across Lion's Den Bluff Trail in this

weather?" blurted Trace.

Wilson sheepishly shrugged as he brushed lank, chilly hair out of his eyes.

"Ain't got the sense to..."

"Oh, you poor dear," cut in Odette. She rushed to Wilson's aid. She flashed her husband the stink eye to try and curb his tongue. He *was* talking to a pastor after all. "Let me take your coat and hat."

As Wilson shed his outer garments, she wrung them out as best she could over her dry sink and placed them where they wouldn't do any further damage to her floors.

"You men go on into the parlor," she said. "I'll have some coffee heated up in just a bit."

"I don't want to put you out any," said Wilson. "I was just hoping the kids were here. This waiting is hard to bear."

"The kids?" exclaimed Trace. "In this weather?" He glared at Wilson as if he was lookin' at a three-legged draft mule. "Tyrone has more sense than to try and cross Rich Mountain in a storm like this."

Spittle gathered at the corner of his mouth.

"And even if he was tempted to try it, he knows I'd

skin him alive for putting my new mare through it."

Odette cringed. She patted her husband on the chest as she walked by, trying in vain to calm him down.

"He's worried about his daughter, dear," she said.

"You think Mr. Colby took them in?" asked Wilson.

"Of course, he did," said Trace, giving his wife a playful swat on the backside as she passed.

Odette immediately reddened and rushed out of the room. Even after all these years, Trace could still make her cringe to her toes with his off-color antics at the most inappropriate times.

"Between the Colby's and the Hannessy's, they got room for the whole bunch of em," Trace continued without a hitch in his dialogue. "I wouldn't be at all surprised if they ain't still kickin' up their heels, havin' the time of their lives. Probably have em a big 'ol breakfast of eggs, tatters, and lamb chops in the mornin' and come moseyin' in here 'round midday or so, blatherin' 'bout what a grand ol' time they had."

A blind man could have seen the relief wash over Wilson's face. *Of course, Trace was right. No one would have tried to traverse those mountains in this weather.*

"And, who knows," continued Trace with a smirk on his face. "If them youngins hit it off really well, maybe us Becketts will be welcomin' a preacher into the family one of these days."

Wilson's heart skipped a beat. Even without the stress of the present situation, that thought alone was apt to keep him sittin' on the edge of his bed the rest of the night.

"Sweet Lord have mercy," he thought.

Upon Odette's insistence that her husband give the pastor a ride home, and Wilson's assurance that it wasn't necessary, they finally settled on an agreeable compromise. Trace would loan the pastor a mule for the trip, and not have to venture out himself.

It was more than Wilson asked, and quite frankly, more than Trace felt was due.

As the clack of iron horseshoes echoed through the dark, Wilson clasped his sodden collar a bit tighter around his neck. Long, boney fingers quivered as a shiver rippled down his lank frame. Though the rains had stopped, the heavy fog it had left behind seemed to seep deep into the man's very bones. A life of pastorin' didn't call for a great deal of time spent out in inclement weather, and he hadn't noticed just how woefully inadequate his outer garments were.

By the time he slipped through the swirling mists that enveloped Brother Greer's outbuildings, he'd decided that was gonna have to change. He'd talk to Delma after service tomorrow morning and see about procurin' the warmest, store-bought heavy coat she could order.

Soon after leaving the Greer ranch behind, its shadowy edifices and darkened windows shrouded in a tomb-like stillness, the pleasant scent of a recently banked hardwood fire drifting over the landscape, he arrived at Baptist Church Road. To a city raised man, even after all these years of living in the Cove, the quiet seemed to assault his senses like a physical force. A malevolent interloper trying in vain to crawl beneath his prickled skin. Only the mournful low of a distant love-sick cow, drifting on the breeze, helped to soothe his frazzled nerves.

Then, as if in reprieve from a clinging malady, he noticed the yellow glow of a far-off shimmering light.

The welcoming luminance of the low-burning oil lamp he had thoughtlessly left ablaze perched atop the frilly cover on his kitchen table. In his hurry to speak with the Becketts, it had been but by the good graces of the Lord Himself, that he hadn't burned his house down.

Love will make a man mighty irresponsible.

Upon arriving home, Wilson eagerly shed his wet clothes and after banking the fire, crawled into bed. Reflecting upon the night's excursion, he couldn't recall a single time he had ever been so mentally and physically exhausted. He pulled his blankets tightly around himself, and let his heavy eyelids sink. His last thoughts before drifting off was a prayer for Mary's well-being. That, and an urgent plea that the Wilsons and the Becketts never become kin.

A deep shiver racked his body that ended in a long, drawn-out snore.

ELEVEN

The Wallow

MARY STARED INTO THE darkness. An overwhelming sense of apprehension gripped her heart. Goosebumps puckered her skin causing the delicate hairs on her arms to stand on end. Something had awakened her from a near comatose state of slumber. A slumber brought on by cold, mental anguish, and physical exhaustion. Her fight-or-flight reflex had been peaked... but she didn't know why.

As she laid in the dirt wallow, beneath the shattered remains of the collapsed roof, she held her breath. Shadows seemed to drift on shadows before her straining eyes. She slowly reached out and tightened her grip on Susan's shoulder.

"No," Susan mumbled as she clutched her blanket tighter and yanked on it, as if to prevent Mary from stealing it.

A board shifted somewhere beyond the roof and clattered among numerous obstacles. It came to rest with a solid thud against the shakes above Mary's head.

Mary winced as dead moss and accumulated dust sprinkled down on her face and into her eyes. Quickly swiping her hand across her brow, she grasped her nose and pursed her lips in a desperate effort not to sneeze. Tears welled as the urge intensified. Dark spots began to float before her eyes as she strained to swallow a large knot developing in her throat.

A sniffing sound, followed by scratching on the weathered shingles made her eyes widen as she slapped her hands over her mouth. She strained to hold back the screech that ripped at her throat.

Whatever was out there, was mere feet away.

The dust, the sneeze, and the knot in her throat were instantly forgotten.

In the darkness, beyond the roof, a snarl was followed by a yelp. That soon led to a cacophony of growls, yaps, and snapping teeth. It sounded as if several animals were shuffling around through the discarded debris of the abandoned cabin. Some apparently laying claim to choice bits of refuse desired by others. Muted barks, snapping jaws, and gnashing teeth accompanied the clatter. A sudden yelp and a squeal led to even more boards and shattered limbs crashing among the ruins.

"What'd you say?" Susan mumbled as she sat up and stretched the cramps out of her shoulders. "It's still dark outside. What are you..."

Mary slapped her hand over Susan's mouth and placed her lips near her ear.

"Shhhh," she hissed. "Something's in the cabin."

Susan, still groggy from sleep and not registering what Mary was trying to tell her, didn't take kindly at all to having a hand full of dirty fingers wrapped tightly around her nose and mouth. She bared her teeth and bit down as hard as she could.

"Ow!" squeaked Mary, snatching her hand away and thrashing it about wildly trying to shake the pain out. Clamping her other hand over her mouth, she tried valiantly not to let loose the peal of agony that was building in her throat. It was nearly unbearable. She'd suffered more anguish in the last thirty-six hours than she had in the previous fifteen years of her life, but nothing compared to the pain of Susan's bite.

About at her wit's end with Susan's attitude, she sat up and pulled back her arm to smack the spoiled brat upside her ear.

A deep grumble stilled her hand and froze her in place.

Lookin' through the dawning light in the makeshift tunnel beneath the roof, she saw a dark shape standing in the opening at the far end. An ebony blob deeper in color than the surrounding shadows. A form that nearly filled the void. The largest coyote she had ever seen.

As her eyes adjusted to the pinpricks of defused light that filtered through the old, tattered shingles, she became aware of bunched shoulders and splayed ears that projected from its lowered head. Of ghostly eyes that glowed white as fire, and of long glistening fangs that ground in snarling jaws.

Grabbing a hand full of Susan's hair, she pulled her face back out of the way to avoid the flailing hands and slashing fingernails. She then forcefully turned the girl's head toward the tunnel and the menace that waited beyond.

Susan froze.

Another blood-curdling growl escaped the beast's heaving chest as an opaque cloud of hot air billowed from its gaping jaws.

"Now, shush," Mary whispered. "We gotta get out of here."

Susan didn't move. The only indication that she had heard at all, was the slight nodding of her head, still clinched tightly in Mary's hand. It was as if the girl couldn't tear her eyes off the creature.

Frantically, glancing around for an exit, Mary saw where the wallow extended under the foundation log of the cabin. During the night, she had been careful to avoid the small chamber beyond because it was saturated with seeping rainwater.

Now, who knows? It may be their only escape.

Slowly crawling to the opening, bein' careful not to make any sudden movements, she slid her head under the wall and looked up at the dripping tangle of wispy roots above. Instead of an ink black void, as she had expected, she saw a multitude of weak, star-like speckles, glaring among the long strands of dangling grass roots. The ground above, having sagged under the weight of last night's deluge was slowly giving way. The sodden soil beneath the newly forming sinkhole had splattered in great plopping clods to the chamber floor below. The resulting canopy of entwined vegetation left numerous cracks and crevasses for daylight to shine through.

Squirming on her back into the cramped space, Mary grimaced as the frigid sludge flowed down her bodice and squished along her spine. Spectral-like fingers of muck massaged the top of her head and oozed like cold oatmeal through her long, matted hair. A three sectioned tap root dropped from above and splattered alongside of her nose before slipping across her lips and chin and settling just above her collar on the front of her neck.

"Yuck," she groaned as she smeared a palm full of slime across her neck, trying to retrieve the clammy tuber.

With an uncontrollable ripple of gooseflesh prickling her skin, and a life-long aversion to filth battling her resolve, she was nearly at her wits end.

After all, she lamented. There's only so much a

girl can endure.

The clamor of snapping jaws and ferocious snarls drifting up the tunnel convinced her she wasn't quite ready to give up just yet.

It's down-right astounding what the human body can endure with the right motivation.

Easing her back into the mud, she raised both legs and pushed her feet into the drooping ceiling. The ground bulged up as a shower of silt and rotten vegetation cascaded down. In an instant she was pelted from head to foot. Turning her face aside, she sputtered and spit trying to displace a strand of muddy grass that had fell across her cheek and lips.

Relaxing her legs, the earth resettled, but stayed in place.

Wiping off her face and arms, she closed her eyes, groaned, and tried again.

"Push!" she spat. "Push! – Push! – Push!"

She strained with everything she had, but to no avail. The tangled mass of overgrown vegetation refused to part. It was interlaced as tight as a sardine fisherman's net and seemed just as strong. Breathing hard, she stared up at the small glints of daylight only an arm's length above her face.

So close, she thought. Oh, so close.

"Aah!" she suddenly hissed in a fit of rage and desperation. Digging both hands deep into the quagmire she was lying in; she began to viciously kick at the drooping ceiling above her. Over and over, she drove her feet into the unrelenting canopy. Over and over, it rose and fell as if mocking her feeble efforts.

Mud and mangled roots bombarded the walls and floor of the small encloser, splattering what few scraps of material Mary had managed to keep dry. With each thrust, her feet sank deeper and deeper into the muck. Yet the overhang remained.

Finally, exhausted, she gave up. She flopped back in the mud, and pressed a grimy fist against her lips trying to hold the sobs in.

"I'm so sorry, Poppa," she whispered. "I tried my best to come home."

A snarl and several yaps interrupted her ruminations. It didn't sound as if the creatures had built up the nerve to charge through the tunnel yet, but it certainly sounded as if there were more of them gathered at the entrance.

Mary doubted that it was a matter of *if* they would attack, but rather of when. And when that time came, what chance did two lone girls stand against beasts of the wild.

A clump of grass and mud slapped Mary on the cheek and splattered across the matted hair on her temple. She jerked back in fright and stared above her. Was the ground giving way? The clump oozed across her temple and settled in her left ear canal.

Terrific, she thought.

Keeping an eye on the overhang, she grimaced as she tried to pluck the blade away.

It wasn't easy.

The grass felt like long, crystalline icicles sharp enough to pierce a pair of canvas snake garters. It was saturated with mud and rot and proved nearly impossible to grasp with her soiled fingers. Try as she might, slip after slip, her half-frozen hands proved to be poor tools for the job.

Turning her left ear toward the ground, she pounded with desperation on her right temple trying to dislodge the blockage.

No luck.

She wiped her finger off on her dress as best she could, then drove it deep into her ear canal. Whatever it took, the obstruction had to go. Leaving it in place was not an option. It was tantamount to having a sliver of stinging nettle lodged beneath your eyelid. Tricky to extract, but impossible to ignore.

Her heart pounded. Her breath caught in her throat. Her sight clouded. And the icy tentacles of panic begin to slither and take root in her overtaxed brain.

Pinching down hard, like a malnourished crawdaddy trying in vain to extract a juicy tadpole from its rocky crevice hideaway, she dug at her quickly reddening earlobe. Her cracked and grime encrusted fingernails scraped and scratched as they tried to find purchase. Her eyes fluttered. Her cheek flinched. A grating sound assaulted her eardrum.

The tangle shifted but stayed firmly in place.

An agonizing pressure began to build in her head. A tear cut a crooked path through the grime on her muddy cheek. Again, and again, she jammed and dug and pinched.

Suddenly, a loud pop exploded behind her eyes.

The pressure vanished. Her hearing cleared. She was thrust into a feeling of bliss.

For a moment.

No sooner did the offending vegetation slip from the throbbing orifice, than the grime and muck clinging to her filthy palm sloughed off and refilled the canal. It was as if one encumbrance dispensed with was recompensed by another.

But in all truth, without the pointy blades of grass scratching against her eardrum, the sludge-like blockage was no more than a minor annoyance.

She laid back her head and sighed with relief.

Looking up, she watched as a two-inch wide gap, six inches long, begin to open in the tangled mass of hanging roots. Daylight flooded into the wallow revealing a cloudless, sunny day. Mary couldn't help but smile.

The gap slowly expanded. The flap of earth drooped. The exit widened.

"Susan," Mary whispered. "Susan, come..."

Suddenly a muddy torrent came flowing into the opening like Ma pitchin' out wash water on laundry day. (All I can figure from the tellin' of it, is a nearby puddle must have dipped with the settlin' earth and poured into the hole).

Mary, not expectin' the deluge, was caught off guard. In an instant, her open mouth was filled with muddy water. She later told me she like t' choked to death, swallerin' about half a gallon of gritty sludge as thick as blackstrap molasses.

As she gagged and sputtered in an uncontrollable fit of coughing, the creatures at the end of the tunnel pulled back and bristled thinkin' the strange sounds were some kind o' challenge. The leader bared his teeth and prepared to meet the threat head on.

"Susan!" Mary gasped between retching hacks.

She winced at the feel of her teeth grinding on clinging clumps of filthy grit. At the same time, she drew a sleeve across her face to wipe away the murky sludge that was draining from her nose.

"Come on, we gotta go."

As the leader of the pack crouched low and began creeping forward, Susan's whole body tensed in a state of near hysterics. An unintentional whimper escaped her throat and a warm sensation spread through the bunched material of her dress below her folded knees. Inch by inch, she involuntarily crawled backward, trying to keep a set distance between herself and impending doom. Not once did she break eye contact with the advancing beast. Not once did she even blink. Her retreat was purely instinctual. Her mind hadn't even registered Mary's plea to escape.

As she drew near the cramped outer chamber of the wallow, Mary scrambled onto her knees trying to make room. Reaching below the cabin's foundation log, she placed her hand on Susan's backside to help guide her to the exit.

Upon contact, Susan let out a shriek of terror and kicked out like o' Cornpone that time he backed his rump into a spiky Honey Locust tree down near Kingston's Flat.

She nearly booted Mary in the face, is what she done.

"Hey!" Mary shouted. "Watch it!"

Susan spun around, still screaming until she recognized Mary for the first time since the stare-down with the beast had begun. Her chest was pounding so hard she feared she was having a heart attack, and by her ghostly pallor, Mary feared she was also.

Meanwhile, unnerved by Susan's piercing scream, the agitated beast in the tunnel leapt back in a panic as if physically struck on the muzzle. Spinning 'round, he collided head-on with his closely following pack members, and flew into an uncontrollable rage, lashing out without mercy. Snarling and growling led to snapping teeth and painful yelps. The clatter of lose boards shifting and dead limbs snapping echoed through the ruins as omega pack members fled the wrath of their alpha leader.

Though social animals by nature, every coyote was innately aware of its role in the pecking order. Great care had to be taken when testing the mettle of their superiors. Any desire to advance required risk. And that risk against the alpha male often led to death. The mountains were strewn with the bones of those who overestimated their potential.

"Come on," Mary coaxed Susan as the snarling continued.

She ground her back deeper into the cold, slimy muck trying to make room for the girl. The limited space in the antechamber offered barely enough room for Mary herself: much less a panic-stricken Susan.

As Susan began to slither into the hole, her hand sank in the morass. She balked.

"What are you doing?" hissed Mary. "Get in here."

Susan remained crouched in place like a great cotton and lace clad praying mantis with one muddy hand held up before her wondering eyes.

"We don't have time for this," pled Mary.

Out of desperation, Mary reached out and grabbed the back of Susan's collar, and with a huff, yanked the girl forward.

Susan literally dove into the chamber, driving the top of her head firmly into the mire on the back wall. The frigid mud oozed around her ears and slid down the back of her dress. Her hands and knees were planted in several inches of liquid slop.

"Eek," she screamed, as she grabbed ahold of Mary's tattered skirt to help pull herself into a standing position. Within moments her expensive party slippers were festooned in clinging mud.

"Now, out!" cried Mary. "Out!"

As Susan rose, her head cleared the edge of the newly formed sinkhole. From that point on, Mary was talking to herself.

Scratching and crawling, kicking and clawing, Susan must have collapsed twenty pounds of mud and yard litter down on Mary as she scurried out of the pit. It didn't even dawn on her that Mary could perhaps use her help as she raced away from the site of her terror.

Mary was on her own.

Nearly as panicked as Susan, Mary prepared to scramble from the chamber when she happened to notice, both blankets were still laying in the dirt where the girls had spent the night.

No reason to think Susan would have taken em.

Only a moment's indecision delayed her before diving into the wallow and plucking the filthy material from the floor. In her rush she bruised her knee on a couple of stone-hard turnips. So much for the feast she'd been anticipating.

When the high-strung, male coyote saw yet another human appear at the end of the tunnel it was more than he could take. With a vicious yowl, he charged. His more dominant pack members fell in close behind.

At the sound of the quickly advancing beasts, Mary yowled herself, and leapt into the waiting antechamber.

If not for the big alpha male being encumbered by the slope of the tilted roof, Mary wouldn't have stood a chance. As it was, she dove out of the hole with the enraged coyote snapping at her heels. His hot breath swept across the back of her leg as his teeth snapped shut mere inches from her ankle. As he toppled back into the pit, he howled with anger at missing his prey. Gathering his feet below him, he prepared to resume the hunt.

Just then, the saturated walls of the sinkhole, weakened by the scrambling exit of the girls, broke loose. Fifty pounds of slush came crashing down on his head and shoulders.

Drenched and saturated in mud, he leapt back from the sudden avalanche, once again plowing headlong into his gathering pack mates.

A rage-fueled melee ensued with all thought of Mary and Susan forgotten. Canines fled as fur and spittle flew.

With sounds of the fight urging her onward, Mary

hurried around the back of the cabin heading for where she had left the horse. If she could only reach it in time, she was sure she could leave her pursuers far behind. Hopefully Susan was there waitin' on her; sittin' bareback and ready to go.

As she rounded the corner, feet slipping in the mud, she suddenly stopped dead in her tracks; her fists clinched.

How could this be?

The horse was gone!

Desperately spinning around in a circle, trying to look everywhere at once, she searched for the mare... for Susan.

Nothing! The clearing was empty!

Hurryin' to the sapling where the horse had been tethered, she stood dumbfounded. The wet vegetation was trampled and scattered with horse droppings. The tree showed scarring where the leather reins had been tied. The grass was ripped and torn by equine teeth. There was no doubt. This was the spot. Susan had ridden off without her.

As howling and yapping picked up once again in the cabin behind her, Mary realized she had no time to lament over her best friend abandoning her. The angry beasts could come pouring out at any moment. She had to go.

A quick glance around revealed an old animal trail next to an overflowing brook that led into the thickets. The path looked dark and spooky, but with coyotes on the loose, one way was as good as another.

Mary tucked the blankets tightly under her arms and fled into the unknown.

TWELVE

Tension

CHARLOTTE AWOKE, HER MIND troubled; her heart racing. A streak of drool was plastered to her cheek like yesterday's hominy and molasses. Her face felt tight and clammy. Scrunching up her nose, she absentmindedly rolled the crusty spittle into a ball with her thumb and forefinger and dropped it onto the cold floor. After a moment, she sat up in bed and pulled her favorite starburst quilt up tight under her chin.

Diver shifted and snorted, chewing on an imaginary apple fritter in his sleep. With a light nudge from Charlotte's foot, he turned over and slipped back into silence once again.

The room was cast in darkness save for a gentle glow from the fireplace Diver had banked as usual before comin' to bed. Only the flicker of muted embers pierced the night. Eerie tendrils of luminance crawled along the pinewood walls like disoriented, translucent caterpillars. Reflections played off a series of adz marks in a ceiling beam that Charlotte often thought resembled an overfed kangaroo.

Outside, the driving rain lashed in waves across the bedroom windows. Thunder rolled on high as streaks of lightning flickered among the treetops. A loose fence board that Diver had yet to mend, clack-clack-clacked in the brisk breeze.

As usual, a myriad of nocturnal sounds played a lullaby for those who chose to listen. Yet, no common night cadence could account for Charlotte's sudden angst. She was a child of the backwoods, and content with the rhythms of nature. Never had she been one to shrink from a bump in the night, or fret at an out-of-place creak beneath the floorboards.

Yet, whatever had awakened her had been like a bolt of apprehension speared through her heart. A sudden lurch from a peaceful slumber to harsh wakefulness. It was an unreasonable but gnawing certainty that something was dreadfully wrong.

Sitting in the dark, she willed her pulse to settle. Her mind to calm. She closed her eyes and tried to comprehend the source of her fears. The harbinger of her dread.

Letting the wind and rain slowly fade into the background, she tried to meld the thunder and clacking boards with the rhythm of her heartbeat. To listen to the silence in between.

The emptiness.

A pop assaulted the stillness as an ember smoldered in the fireplace. The crinkling of rag pulp paper betrayed a white-footed mouse as it scurried across a credit voucher resting on Diver's writing desk. The gurgle of a well-fed stomach attested to her husband's contentment. A congested cough drifted out of the darkness.

Charlotte held her breath.

A wheeze as soft as a newborn kitten's sigh.

Pauline?

"Pauline!" yelped Charlotte.

In a tizzy, she threw back her quilt and leapt from her bed. Racing barefooted across the eight feet of sand rubbed floorboards, she reached Pauline's bassinet. Diver was right behind her.

Pauline's tiny face was imperceptible in the dark, but a high-pitched wheeze as she tried to inhale cut like death's own reaping scythe through Charlotte's heart.

"What is it?" asked Diver. "What's happened?"

Diver was in the habit of sleeping in a low fitting cap to ward off painful earaches brought on by the cold night air. (The aftereffects of the plunge he'd takin' over them falls, years ago.) Because of his compromised hearing, he wasn't aware of Pauline's plight.

"Pauline," cried Charlotte picking the child up and cradling her as she returned to sit on the side of her bed. "She can't breathe!"

Diver quickly stoked the embers into life and threw another log on the fire. He then used a homemade spill to light his new Argand lantern.

As he lowered the narrow glass chimney over the cylindrical wick, light spilled forth driving long wavering shadows across the room. Ghostly silhouettes of bedposts, a coatrack, and Charlotte's spinning wheel all played along the far walls.

Condensation on rain-washed windowpanes glistened with a thousand points of reflected light. The previously quiet and tranquil room had suddenly become menacing and surreal.

But the sight that threatened to bring Diver to his knees was the spectral-like image of Charlotte and Pauline as it was cast on the wall beyond the bed. A sight so ingrained in his mind, his breath hitched in his throat and his heart chilled as if on ice. It was the identical scene of his remembrance that played out in young Dennis' room the night his world collapsed.

The night he thought he would surely die.

With a start, reality crashed down on him like a maul through hickory firewood.

This isn't Dennis, he thought. This is Pauline. My sweet Pauline.

Rushing to Charlotte's side, he said, "Give her to me."

Charlotte let her tears flow freely as she eased her laboring daughter from her shoulder and handed her over to the only man on earth that she trusted with all her heart.

"Lord, help us," Diver prayed as he laid Pauline

face down on his left forearm with two fingers on each side of her tiny neck. He then dipped her head toward the floor and began patting her back with his right hand, beginning just below the ribs and continuing up to her shoulder blades.

"Don't take my Pauline too," he pleaded.

Three times, he repeated his ministrations. Each time using restraint so as not to harm the child in his excitement. Then, on the third try, Pauline's little chest heaved, and with a wet, retching sound, a thin stream of pale-yellow fluid came flowing from her gaping mouth.

"Thank you, Lord," Diver uttered as he softly continued to massage the back of her clinging, sweat dampened nightshift.

Even as the spew pooled around Diver's bare feet, Pauline gave a big gasp, sneezed clotted mucus from her button nose, and began wailing like a love-sick loon on a moonless night.

Charlotte and Diver had never heard a lovelier refrain in their entire lives.

Reaching out, Charlotte took her weeping baby from Diver's hands and gently hugged her to her breast. Tears flowed freely down her face as she cried right along with her daughter.

Diver didn't mind at all. As the cold rain continued to lash the windows, and the loose board continued the clack as if applauding a job well done, he stood barefoot in the quickly cooling puddle. His glistening eyes said it best; the tears of relief and joy were a family affair.

Come Sunday mornin' me and Pa stood drinkin' coffee on the front porch as we surveyed last night's storm damage to the homestead.

"The Lord sure dropped us a mess o' firewood," he said.

"Yes, sir, I reckon He did," I answered

The front yard was scattered with fallen limbs and mounds of debris that had washed down from the hillside. More than a few moss-covered shake shingles that had once perched atop the cabin roof were now strewn about, being picked over by Ma's chickens.

A large oak tree had uprooted taking out part of Ma's garden fence, and the south wall of the chicken coop. A man-sized branch had planted itself dead center of her pea patch.

It kinda tickled me some is what it done, lookin' for the whole world like a big ol' one-armed scarecrow with a spiky hairdo.

I shook my head and chuckled.

Reckon Pa didn't see the humor in the situation. He looked at me a bit strange, but didn't say anything.

It was just then that a voice beckoned from behind us, "Quite a gully washer last night!"

We turned to see Casey clammerin' along the barn apartment's flagstone walkway. He'd inherited the dwelling back when Diver and Charlotte built their new place and moved down to the Cove.

Fact is, I thought I'd be gettin' it myself, but seein's how he was my older brother, I didn't begrudge him none.

From the look of things, it appeared he'd stepped in a pile of muck right about the time he'd called out to us and was presently doin' what he could to shake it loose. Showin' some mighty fancy dance steps in the process too, if ya was to ask me. Course, I had to smile, knowin' how Ma had threatened to throw his breakfast out next time he showed up late cause o' stayin' out with Thelma till all hours. Said she'd give it to Baby and have done with it.

Truth be told, with the way Casey hankered for Ma's breakfast vittles, I ain't real sure which one of 'em would o' won the tussle even if she had; the lovesick salt tycoon, or the hen whipped coonhound.

Pa gave me a wink as Casey clack, squish, clack, squished his way across the bridge. I reckon he was just as tickled by Ma layin' down the law as I was.

"Yep," he said as Casey drew near. "Quite a blow."

Pa sipped from his hot mug and grimaced.

"Heard ya come in durin' the wee hours this mornin'," he said. He plucked a flake of grounds from the tip of his tongue and flicked it away. "Figured I'd be askin' Billy's dog if she preferred eggs or flapjacks for breakfast this mornin'."

Casey 'bout missed the step as he clambered onto the porch, but he wisely chose not to take the bait Pa was tossin'.

"Yeah, that squall slowed us down a bit crossin' Rich Mountain," he said, wipin' his soiled shoes on the reed mat Ma kept on the front stoop. "Laid a tree 'cross the far end o' Baptist Church Road too. We had to go plumb back past Forrest's place to get around it."

He flipped the corner of the mat up on its side with his right foot tryin' to use it to scrape clean the muddy sides of his other shoe.

As far as I could see, he wasn't doin' nothin' but makin' a bigger mess.

"Surprised ya heard me come in with all that racket goin' on," he said to Pa. "Sorry if I woke ya."

Pa watched Casey muddy up Ma's mat. At best he was turning clumps to globs, and globs to smears. It was kinda like watchin' a fella try to bail out a sinking boat with a bottomless bucket. Before long, he gave up, pulled his shoes off, and opting to go barefoot rather than chance marring Ma's clean floors.

"Don't sleep real sound these days," Pa said as he massaged the side of his neck. "This bum shoulder o' mine gets my fingers t' tinglin' so bad I feel like I got ants in bed with me. Seems like my breathin' ain't so good at night either."

Me and Casey both looked at Pa a bit concerned.

"Aw, it ain't nothin'," he said. "Maybe comin'

down with the grippe or somethin'. I don't reckon I'm ready to be put out to pasture just yet."

Baby ambled over and sniffed at Casey's filthy shoes as if questioning their presence on her porch. Once determining they weren't edible, and perhaps not all that pleasant to sniff at either, she let em be. Yawning, she dropped off the end of the porch and trotted off towards the woods.

"Off to make her rounds, I reckon," said Pa.

We both knew she'd soon be sniffin' out every move any critter had made in her domain during the dark of night.

"Anyway," Pa continued. "We better be gettin' in there and eat before your Ma makes good on her promise and pitches the whole kit and caboodle out to the hogs. I sure admire me a happy hog, but not if he's eaten better than I am."

As Casey nudged the mat to the side with his foot, he said, "I'll get this mess cleaned up before church."

"Yes, you will," said Pa. He then clasped both of us by the shoulder and ushered us into the house.

"When ya hitch the team up for church after your choirs," he said to me, "pitch the axes and bucksaw in the wagon. We'll clear that roadway after services."

"Yes, sir," I said.

That was Pa for ya. We seldom even used that part of Baptist Church Road, yet there he was, fixin to clear it for those that did.

Can't say that would o' happened back before Diver came along.

≈

Tyrone awoke feelin' like someone had filled his head full of cockleburs. His temples throbbed, his eyelids were crusted over with gritty mucus, and his throat felt like he'd swallowed a barn sized hive of angry yellow jackets. Even his hair hurt.

If this is what the 'good stuff' feels like, he thought as he sat head in hand, elbows on his knees, I sure hope I never get ahold of true rotgut.

With a stench wafting off his soiled shirt, and the residue of sour mash coating his teeth and tongue, he cautiously rose and went in search of cold water.

Never again, he lamented. Just let me survive and I'll never touch that stuff again.

Pushing through a sagging pinewood door that

screeched like a pen full of porkers at slopping time, he paused on the rickety porch of the cabin he'd spent the night in. It creaked and swayed with his weight.

Grasping a shaky handrail, he grimaced as he gagged, but managed to swallow down the rising bitter swill. His stomach churned as a burning sensation seared the back of his throat. A groan escaped as he wiped away beads of sweat and dirty tear tracks on his cheeks.

Finally, feeling a bit steadier, he squinted out at the silent aftermath of last evening's festivities.

A thousand water-droplets glistened on the lawn in the early morning sun, creating a shimmering vista of lights that hurt his eyes. Sparrows chased flying insects through the massive rafters of the open-faced barn where the celebration had taken place. Its broad, rough-hewn dance floor now laid strewn with several upturned benches and mismatched drinking vessels that seemed to have been forgotten and left scattered about. Even an occasional scarf or bonnet peeked out among the tangled debris.

Near the roadway a single, royal-blue dancing slipper rested in the mud.

How could someone lose their shoe? he wondered.

Dogs sniffed and scratched through the scattered refuse in search of leftover food scraps. Whenever a discarded morsel *was* found, a brisk scuffle was sure to follow. Loyalty among the pack extended to territory and protection from outsiders, but not sustenance.

The fields were scattered with water buckets, and the tangled grasses trampled and torn as if by a myriad of hastily departing conveyances. Iron rimmed wagon wheels had left great swirling arches imprinted in the muddy ground.

Probably trying to outdistance the storm, Tyrone thought. As he stood there contemplating, he realized that though he knew it had stormed, he couldn't actually remember the deluge itself.

"Strange," he uttered.

Hearing a soft, gurgling sound, he turned his head and noticed a picturesque, rock-strewn stream nestled in a shadowy wood line not far from the cabin.

Water!

Massaging his temples, he carefully climbed down

the warped cabin steps and ambled off toward the life-giving flow. Even as he walked, something about the abandoned grassy field he'd been studyin' made his innards clinch, and his headache spike. Something of import, but for the life of him he couldn't figure what.

As he neared the stream, he removed his foul-smelling shirt and dropped it into a quiet eddy, leaving it to swirl in the trapped current. He then laid on his stomach and gingerly submerged his pounding head into the soothing waters. His breath caught; his ears flared. A searing pain ingulfed his teeth.

"Brrrr," he sputtered.

As he fought the urge to pull back, his bare skin bristled with waves of tingling gooseflesh. Bubbles streamed past his ears. It was all he could do to remain in place, but he knew he needed to let the healing waters do their job.

Within moments the pounding pressure in his skull eased. Relief engulfed him. He had an inkling of hope; he might survive. Sucking in a mouthful of water he sat up and let the refreshing fluid dribble down his raw throat.

Suddenly the image of crystalline water washing away massive heaps of decaying sheep waste in a pasture further upstream invaded his mind.

Be just my luck, he contemplated. *Survive the corn mash and die of the Tennessee Trots.* He gagged as a bit of water went down the wrong pipe.

"Ol' Doc Dulaney ain't gonna know what to tell Pa done me in," he mused. "Poison corn mash, stream borne meadow muffins, or drownin' while chucklin'."

Sitting up, he laughed as he reached over and swirled his shirt around in the eddy. He was pleased to see the stream had carried away the lion's share of the filth. Pickin' it up, he wrung it out and gave it a good flick to displace the dripping water.

"Not bad," he said to himself. "Maybe not up to Ma's standards, but close enough."

Standin', he clutched the shirt in the ball of his fist. Remainin' wrinkle-free wasn't high on his list. Figured Ma'd make a point of rewashin' the thing before he wore it again anyway.

"Now, where are those cousins of mine?" he muttered, pressin' the cold material to his forehead.

The last thing he could remember was a blurry-faced stranger pullin' him from the dancefloor and throwing him into Trey and Gary's arms.

"Time you boys took your party someplace else," the fella had muttered. "Go find yourself a quiet retreat where ya can sleep it off."

At the time, that seemed like the funniest thing he'd ever heard. They'd stumbled away into the dark, arm in arm; one more unsteady than the next.

"Is this a quiet retreat?" sneered Gary.

"No, I think that's a quiet retreat over there," quipped Trey.

Tyrone hadn't said anything. Quite frankly, the way his stomach was roiling, he was afraid of what might come out if he opened his mouth.

"I think this'll do," said Gary as they stood swayin', arm in arm. They were standing before a small, decrepit cabin at the edge of the woods. "Uncle Lim's hideaway."

"Where Lim went when Aunt Betty threw him out for stinkin' so bad every shearin' season," said Trey. "She never did catch on that he kept his sqeezin's in here and didn't bathe just so she'd run him off the way she done."

"Course, I wasn't but a kid," said Gary, "but what I remember 'bout Aunt Betty, I'd a runned off too, mash or no."

They all laughed at that.

It took the boys four attempts to successfully climb the three rickety steps to the just-as-rickety porch. They then shushed one another as they forced open the loudly creaking door.

"You're the guest." Gary told Tyrone. "Pick your abode."

There was an old sagging cot, a pile of filthy gunny sacks, and a half-full tub of seed corn scattered across the dirty floor. Tyrone flopped down on the cot and hadn't seen a soul since.

Headin' back toward the cabin, he hadn't taken four steps when... "Pa's horse and buggy!" he gasped. That's what was missin'. "I left Pa's horse and buggy right there in the field, but they're gone!"

At a head jarring trot, he hurried to the exact spot where he had anchored the blood bay mare.

Gone! He thought. *Gone!*

Twistin' around, frantically glancing this way and that, he desperately searched the surrounding area as if the rig might magically reappear. It didn't.

His knees weakened. His pulse throbbed. His innards flip-flopped. With no warning whatsoever, bile burned the lining of his stomach and erupted up his throat. A groan rent his chest even as he spewed into the tall grass.

"What have I done?" he moaned. Tears moistened his red-rimmed eyes. "Pa's gonna skin me sure."

He stood there, bent at the waist, hands clasping his head as if to keep it from exploding. His heart was thumping so hard he could feel it pounding in his temples. If there was one thing he knew beyond all doubt, it was Pa ain't one to listen to excuses. The rig was his responsibility; he'd be payin' the piper.

"Hey cuz, what ya up to?"

Jumpin' at the sound, Tyrone turned to see Gary and Trey leadin' saddled horses from a nearby corral.

"We gotta go check on the sheep up on Dunkin Field," Gary said. "Kenny Gladson claims he saw some coyotes up that way and Pa thinks we might aught a drive the flock down a little closer. Says the women folk 'round here's coddled them dogs so much they won't spend no time up on the bald knobs like they's supposed to."

Dashing forward, Tyrone pushed Gary aside. He then grabbed the reins to his horse and climbed astride.

"Gotta borrow your horse," he declared.

"Now, wait a minute," Gary protested. "You can't just up and take a man's horse..."

"No time," shouted Tyrone, giggin' the sorrel into a fast trot, then a full gallop. "I gotta go!" As he raced across the field, he called in a voice too jarred to be understood, "I'll get her back to ya as soon as I can."

Gary pulled his hat from his head and flung it on the ground. He never had figured Tyrone Beckett for havin' a lick of since, but to flat-out steal a man's horse?

"Did you see that?" Gary blurted at Trey. "He stole Pa's best workin' horse."

Trey snickered. "Sure glad I'm not the one whose gonna have to tell your Pa I can't hold onto my own horse. Must be downright humiliatin' to be so faint-hearted."

With that, Trey climbed atop his filly before Gary had a chance to throttle him. As he turned toward

216

Dunkin Field he called, "Catch up as soon as you can. I ain't figurin' on doin' all the work around this place my ownself."

Gary stood flabbergasted. One cousin ridin' off to do the job his pa had told him to do, and the other hightailin' it for Cades Cove atop Pa's favorite mount.

What more could this day bring?

THIRTEEN

The Chestnut Haint

MARY TUMBLED HEADFIRST OVER the leading edge of a towering cliff face. Grasping and shrieking, she frantically tried to arrest her slide as she neared the void eighteen feet below. The vista beyond seemed to grow at an incredible pace as it rushed toward her face. Then, miraculously, at the last possible moment, the far-reaching tendrils of a Virgina Creeper brought her to an abrupt stop. She was mere inches from a harrowing, hundred and thirty-foot drop. The tendrils, far too weak to support a full-grown girl, stretched and snapped. Loose gravel shifted beneath her outstretched palms trickling over the crumbling edge. If not for small protrusions in the rain-slick slope that she managed to find purchase on, she would surely have been thrust to the rugged boulders and shadowy fissures far below.

With a painful catch in her throat, she stared out across the open expanse that laid before her. Her innards clinched. Death had once again came courting. But for the will of God, she feared she'd never survive this ordeal.

Slowly, she began inching her way around to get her head facing uphill. Tears coursed down her cheeks as she desperately grappled with the unstable greenery. For every foot of altitude she acquired, she paid the price with a heart-stopping slippage of several inches. Time and again, she cast away useless handfuls of weakened undergrowth only to drive her bruised and bleeding fingers deeper into the foliage for a more secure grip. With each grasp a new trickle of pebbles cascaded past her outstretched body.

All morning long, she had raced through hostile backwoods, frantically trying to leave the cabin of terrors as far behind as possible. Her once beautiful and cherished social gown now hung tattered and torn after hours of dashing through large patches of thorny wait-a-minute brush with reckless regard. Her silky blond hair hung filthy, and briar tangled, loose and matted as it flapped in the breeze. Where her bonnet had gotten to, she had no idea.

The only thing that protected her hands and arms from being shredded on the sickle-like barbs were the two mud-caked blankets she still held clutched to her breast. Somehow, the thought of letting them go seemed tantamount to defeat.

That was until she barreled through a thick stand of flowering ironweed and suddenly found herself tumbling free through the thin air. As she frantically gyrated across the seemingly endless void before coming to a most unglamorous stop, the blankets were released and vanished into the abyss. If not for the clinging vegetation, she would have joined them.

Now, gasping for air, and nearly hysterical with fear, she gave one last desperate lunge as she dug her shoeless feet deep into the gravely surface of the mountain. To her horror, the loose scree beneath her shifted, then gave way. The entire hillside began to move. She was falling!

With a scream of terror and desperation, she flung her arms out and wildly flailed about for any secure surface she could grab.

Pain flared through her right wrist, but amazingly her descent came to a jarring halt. Looking up, she saw that her hand was wedged between two protruding boulders. Even as the last of the loose rocks tumbled into the unknown, her agonizing hold anchored her in place. Blood oozed from her bruised and torn forearm, but she cried and cheered in equal measure at her sudden salvation.

Riding a high of nervous energy and overwhelming relief, she soon had herself pulled to safety on the lip of the ridge. She laid back and clutched her arm to her chest as she let the tears flow.

"You ain't gettin' no meal here today!" she snapped at a large turkey vulture as it hovered high overhead.

Sometimes it felt like everything in the mountains was out to get ya.

As time passed, and Mary's breathing settled, a light breeze played across the delicate hairs on her exposed arms. A slight chill rippled down her spine. She shivered. The coming night was sure to be cold. All the more reason to regret losing her blankets. Sitting up, she suddenly winced in pain. In the relief of surviving the rockfall, she'd forgotten about her damaged arm. How that could be, she hadn't a clue.

Looking at the swollen, quickly darkening flesh of her right wrist, she grimaced. It didn't look good. She tried to open and close her fist. A sharp pain flared from fingertip to elbow.

"Ow, that hurt!" she moaned.

Throwing her head back, she gently rocked in place, cradling her tender arm to her chest until the throbbing pain eased. Then, gritting her teeth, she tried flexing her hand once again. This time, duly forewarned of the impending agony, everything seemed to work.

She didn't think it was broken.

As she sat contemplating her fate, she reasoned her most immediate concerns were, soaking the arm in cold water to reduce the swelling, finding a clear stream to quench her thirst, and recovering the lost blankets before nightfall set in.

As for food, she had eaten one of the bitter turnups found growing wild in the abandoned garden as she fled through the wilderness. The other had been lost on the rockslide. From the way her stomach churned, she didn't feel she'd be eating anything else soon.

To accomplish her three main goals, she needed to find a way off that mountain. Preferably without breaking her neck in the process.

Taking care not to jostle her injured right arm, she used her left hand, with the welcome aid of a nearby sapling, to rise. From her vantage-point atop the ridge she could see for miles. Nothing but knob after knob, clothed in the most spectacular fall colors; interspersed by long sweeping hollows as far as the eye could see.

Great blanketing shadows slowly drifted across the woodland peaks and valleys mimicking the course of billowing clouds above. Far in the distance the soaring turkey vulture was joined by a traveling companion as they glided away in search of deceased delicacies to eat.

Looking to the south, the rugged terrain and bare-faced cliff stretched out as far as she could see. A half-mile to the north the mountain dropped off in a series of woody terraces to the valley below.

Mary turned north.

After seemingly being plagued by trouble with every step she took, Mary held out little hope that the descent to the valley floor would be as easy as it appeared from above. She assumed she'd be greeted by hidden drop-offs, massive growths of stinging nettles, and perhaps an angry rattlesnake to boot. Why should things be any different now? So it was with great shock, and immense pleasure, that within an hour of starting her trek north, she was standing on the bank of a small, spring-fed pond at the base of the declivity. No broken bones, no plant based festering rashes, and no weeping puncture wounds dripping with agonizing snake venom.

Maybe everything in the mountains weren't out to get her after all.

Easing to her knees, she bunched up her long skirt to use as a cushion against the gravely shoreline, then bent forward to sip a mouthful of cold, tooth-chilling water. Her tonsils burned as the frigid liquid trickled down her throat. Never had she hurt so fine.

After quenching her thirst, she settled down on her left hip and gently lowered her swollen arm into the pool. Several startled minnows, oblivious to the

world of giants beyond their watery realm, left
swirling streaks of ocher colored sediment in their
wake as they dashed for the far shore. A speckled,
black crayfish tucked his six-segmented tail tight
under his body as he backed away with open claws
extended as if warning her to stay away.

Even as she chuckled at the feisty little
crustacean, she had to bite her lower lip when the
healing waters began doing their work. Small tendrils
of pink from several torn and ruptured abrasions
drifted away on the current as it flowed down a stone
strewn spillway to a leaf clogged brook below. Searing
pain engulfed her mangled flesh as distressed nerve
endings came in contact with the bitter cold. Several
anxious moments passed before the pain finally began
to subside. When it did, blessed numbness took its
place.

Mary breathed a sigh of relief and sat back resting
the dripping appendage in her lap. It may have simply
been wishful thinking, but she was sure the swelling
had gone down some. In a spurt of hesitant
trepidation, she steeled her nerves and tried to flex
her fingers. They responded with only the slightest of

pain. Elation welled in her soul.

Carefully crawling to a nearby tree, she leaned her back against it and raised her face to the warm rays of the afternoon sun. The heat felt good playing across her cheeks. The dull pain in her arm throbbed but was mostly forgotten. She closed her weary eyes and soon drifted off into a much-needed slumber. For a little while, her tribulations were forgotten.

It was then that a rather plump, but crafty fox squirrel who had taken refuge on the back side of the tree, decided to scamper away across an overhanging branch. Though its way seemed to be barred by a wind-swept tangle of dry, twisted foliage, it clambered through without a moment's hesitation. A small cache of rainwater, gathered in the wilted leaves, spilled out and dribbled from the limb.

Mary, with the help of Sarah May, had just presented her father with a large bowl of raspberry ice cream and sponge cake for his birthday. It was a joyous occasion. Everyone in the Cove had gathered to celebrate the event.

Suddenly she was ripped from her dream.

Flinching, she thrust her left hand to her matted

hair. A yelp quickly followed as she absentmindedly used her right to sit up a bit straighter. It didn't take long to remember her injury.

Hugging her once again throbbing hand to her chest, she grimaced as her eyes began to swell.

"What's going on?" she moaned.

Being so abruptly yanked from a tender and heart-warming fantasy only to be thrust back into the shock of reality was nearly more than she could endure. After brushing her hair out with her fingers, she sat back and quizzically looked at her hand.

It was wet!

Suddenly a muck...muck...muck sound came from above. She looked up.

A fat, red-coated squirrel, furiously flicked his long bushy tail as he scampered away. In two quick leaps he disappeared behind a stout, twisted limb.

"Oh no, you didn't," Mary hissed as she gingerly plucked a thick strand of sodden hair away from her damp left ear. Suddenly, the whole mountain was against her once again.

After several minutes of dabbing at the soiled locks with a handful of wild grass and dried leaves,

Mary crawled back to the pond to resoak her injured hand. The pain thankfully eased much sooner this time. The little pond really did seem to have healing waters.

Then, after takin' another soothing drink, Mary seriously contemplated washin' out her filthy, much abused tresses. Even in frigid water, it was certainly tempting.

After all, a girl doesn't exactly feel her best walkin' around with a head full of 'squirrel dew', she reasoned. But then again, the thought of spendin' the night with wet, clammy hair wasn't at all appealing. As disgusting as it was, she'd have to wait till mornin' to do anything about it.

With that settled, she realized it was about time to go find her lost blankets. Wet hair or not, she had no desire to cuddle down with nothing but dried leaves for protection against the night's chill. What Susan was gonna do to keep warm, she had no idea. But it served her right. How could she have run off like that, leaving her best friend stranded with a pack of angry coyotes and no horse to get away on?

When I find that girl! she thought.

Rising, Mary picked up a long stick and began prying spy holes in the underbrush. Within minutes she found a game trail that led in the direction she wanted to go. Glancing both ways, a shiver ran down her spine. The trail, following the cliff base, was cloaked in shadows ... musty and dank. Not at all appealing to a young girl's sensibilities. But then again, it was the only avenue of travel available.

Steeling her nerve, she ducked under a low-hanging limb and followed the trail, brushing back soggy foliage as she went. At the very least, the annoying muck...muck of the bothersome squirrel gradually faded into the distance.

After a while the canopy above thinned, and shafts of sunlight speckled the forest floor. Colorful songbirds flittered about, tweeting and chirping as she passed.

This isn't so bad, she thought.

Then, as if to quash any feeling of contentment she might have, she heard a long, drawn-out sound, reverberating off the towering bluff-face; *Ayeee ... Arrreee.*

It was downright creepy, is what it was. As it

echoed through the hardwoods even the birds paused in their merriment.

"What was that?" Mary gasped.

Looking about, she realized the forest was suddenly deathly quiet. Wide-eyed and frightened, she picked up her pace, anxious to distance herself from the scene. Even thorns and snags failed to be impediments. She simply swatted them to the side and ambled through.

Before long, Mary noticed a shadowy figure silhouetted in the lower branches of a large chestnut tree. It just hung there, in mid-air, hovering several feet above the ground. Its form was unlike anything she had ever seen before. It slowly swayed and twisted as if keeping close watch over the surrounding scrub; unwilling to let any intruder approach unnoticed.

Mary quickly scrambled over a fallen log and took refuge behind a large boulder. She had no idea if she'd been spotted. Her breathing erratic. Her heartbeat so loud she was sure it would give her away.

What is that thing? she pondered. It certainly isn't human. Could that be what they call a haint?

Crouched low, knees wedged firmly to her chest,

hands over her face, Mary tried to make herself as small as possible. Whatever it was, she figured it was probably just as hostile as everything else in these backwoods.

Oh, please. I just want to go home, she pleaded.

Snap!

What was that?

A sharp exhalation of air; not from herself — but from it!

Several seconds passed as she held her breath. She had to clamp her jaws tight to keep her teeth from rattling. An errant dribble of mucus dampened her upper lip.

A soft shuffle and crackle of dry leaves crushed under foot advanced toward her refuge. A sniff and scrape followed by a distinct crackling sound. A dry cough. A quiver of brush. Over the span of ten minutes, sounds slowly grew. They drew closer. Some mere feet beyond her boulder. Some off to her left. She struggled with every ounce of resolve in her being not to cry out in panic.

Suddenly, a small tree began violently shaking. A grating noise rent the stillness. It sounded as if the bark was being stripped from its trunk.

Unnerved, she spun toward the impending peril. Her peripheral vision caught movement to her left. Her ears registered sounds to her right. She shrieked and tried to look both ways at once.

With a sudden commotion, a whitetail doe nearly flipped over backward in her hurry to flee the area. Her tail raised high flashed a warning to every deer in the area.

Looking back to her right, Mary caught the fleeting glimpse of a large buck as it silently bound away into a thick stand of lodgepole pine. As only a whitetail can do, it simply vanished into the woodlot. Not a waisted motion, nor the snap of a twig.

Everything had happened so quickly it was more of an image flashed before her eyes than a real-life event.

Mary sat back gulping in cool air as she let heart rate settled for the second time that day.

Wonder how many years that just cost me, she mused.

With the giddiness of suddenly released angst, she couldn't help but grin.

"If Billy could only see me now. He'd die laughing at what a scaredy-cat I am," she chuckled.

But even as she rallied a new terror gripped her heart. She'd forgotten about the spectral figure in the tree. How it had hovered there in plain sight; keeping watch as if ready to pounce on any wayward passers.

There's no way them deer could have not seen it, she mused. Why hadn't they been frightened away?

Lying flat on her stomach, she slowly edged her way forward. If she could only peek around the base of the boulder without being seen.

Perhaps the creature has already left, she pondered. Or maybe it's a protector, not a menace. It might even be friendly.

Maybe? Perhaps? But why take chances? After all, a haint was a haint in Mary's mind. And in all her years, she'd never heard of a benevolent haint.

No, she wasn't falling for that ruse.

Remembering the subtle rustling of leaves and twigs the deer had made in their foraging, Mary took care to gently pluck up and place aside every scrap of debris that may have crackled as she inched forward. That being accomplished, she slowly edged up to a crack in the rock until her line of sight came in contact with the specter's tree.

She froze.

With the advancement of the afternoon sun, a ray of brilliant light had spilled through a 'V' shaped craig in the towering cliff above. Its beam had settled directly on the lower portions of the old chestnut tree. A golden glow defused the gloom. There, in the center of the radiance, flapping in the wind like a living menace, hung one of Mary's filthy blankets. It was suspended from a slender, nearly invisible twig. Though unexceptional, and certainly benign to a backwoods trapper or grizzled mountain man, the effect had been harrowing to Mary; an impressionable young lady not accustomed to traveling the wilds alone. Not that a person could fault her for it, mind you. If truth be told, there's a whole heap o' haints talked about 'round the campfire. The teller just seems to forget about mentionin' that on closer inspection, it was only a blanket.

Mary dropped her head on her arms and laughed till she cried. If only she could crawl out of this nightmare and see her home again. Feel her father's hug and hear me tell her I forgive her for going to the dance with Tyrone. Oh, how she wanted to say how truly sorry she was.

If she ever did find her way home, she knew she'd forever be a stronger person. Never again would she lower her standards for pride or pity. Never again would she quiver in the face of the unknown. Never again, no matter how compelling the illusion, would she kowtow before a toothless threat. A menace like the one she'd always remember as "the chestnut haint". Or so she told herself.

FOURTEEN

Calamity Rising

PASTOR WILSON, AFTER LEADING his congregation in an inspirational rendition of the hymn, "Come Thou Almighty King", placed his dog-eared Bible on the lectern, and looked out across the gathering. As usual, it was heart-warming to see so many of his flock present to receive the Lord's word.

A true blessing is what it is, he thought.

He marveled at how these hard-workin', God-fearin', mountain folks, had welcomed a big-city, flat-lander and his daughter into their hearts and homes all those years ago. How they had accepted him as their friend, confidant, and spiritual leader.

But on this crisp, Sunday mornin', there was a noticeable absence in the throng. The pew where Diver and Charlotte McCoy customarily sat was empty.

Wilson couldn't remember a single service without Diver sittin' front row, left side. Unless, that is, he was on the pulpit, giving the lesson.

Knowin' how close the Banions and McCoys were, he looked half-way down the sanctuary to see me sittin' on the righthand side of the aisle along with Ma, Pa, and Delma. Little J.J. was in my lap playin' with a sawdust filled, leather bunny rabbit.

James wasn't present, as usual.

Casey and Thelma sat directly behind us, and the entire third pew on the left side was occupied by Forrest's clan.

Odd, the pastor thought. *The Banions present, but not the McCoys?* He made a mental note to check on Diver and Charlotte's welfare after services.

Thumbing the first reference tab in his Bible for this morning's message, he looked out and smiled at the upturned faces.

"Isn't it a wonderful morning?" he said.

"Yes, it is," retorted Mable Davis to the chuckles of several congregants.

It was then that it stuck him.

What's Casey and Thelma doing here? Why aren't they at the Colby-Hannessy farm with the other stranded party goers. If they're here, where's Mary?

Quickly glancing around, he saw Miss Shelly sittin' in the front row with Dean and Lidia Tudwell.

"Sister Shelly," he said, "would you be so kind as to come up and lead us in a chorus of "Amazing Grace?"

As a startled Miss Shelly came forward, Wilson hurried down the aisle and quietly asked Casey to follow him outside.

"Sure, Preacher," he said bewildered.

The men went out front and stood near Casey's weathered salt wagon. Casey fished an apple from his pocket and offered it to his mammoth mule. A habit he'd picked up from Pa.

"What can I do for ya, Preacher?"

"Did you and your party come across Rich Mountain in that storm last night by yourselves?" Wilson asked.

"No," said Casey. "The whole lot of us came back together. Weren't so bad when we started out, but by the time we reached the Cove, we knew we'd got us a wettin', I can tell ya."

"Did Mary and Tyrone come back with ya?"

"No," said Casey. "They left before we did."

"Before?" sputtered Wilson. "Why would they leave before?"

Casey realized something was amiss.

"Well, I guess that might not be quite right," he said. "I didn't witness it myself, but I heard there was some kind of a ruckus on the dance floor and Mary and Susan Beckett hurried off with a young fella from Tuckaleechee Cove. I figured they just went outside to let things cool down."

He brushed his hair back and got a pained look on his face.

"But a bit later, word spread that they rode off with Trace Beckett's rig and prized mare leaving Tyrone behind to fend for hisself."

"But you don't know where they went?" asked Wilson.

"I figured they went home," said Casey. "It looked like a storm was brewin', so we all bundled up and headed out shortly after that ourselves. I have no idea what happened with Tyrone. Nobody could find him.

Course, with the Colbys and Hennessys bein' his kin anyway, we didn't give all that much thought. Figured they'd see to it that he got home if need be."

"But the girls definitely did not leave with you?" Wilson queried.

"No, Preacher," Casey said, shaking his head and rubbing at a hot sensation building on the back of his neck. Something wasn't right, and he was gettin' mighty uncomfortable. "Like I said, they left before we did. I figured we'd come across em somewhere along the way, but they must have been in quite a hurry, cause we never did catch up to em."

He pulled his hand from the back of his neck and scratched at the day-old stubble on his chin. He hadn't had time to shave that morning due to havin' to clean Ma's muddy porch off.

"Why, what happened?" he asked.

"Mary never came home last night." Wilson said with a catch in his throat. "I don't know where she is!"

Casey was dumbfounded. He thought back on the trip home. They'd watched out for the girls the whole way, but knowing they'd a good head start, didn't think much of not catchin' up to em. On the other hand, that storm *was* awful bad. Could they have went off the road and been missed completely?

By then, several parishioners had come outside to see what the problem was. It wasn't like Brother Wilson to walk out on his own service.

"Mary's missing?" blurted Edith Blyth as she grabbed the pastor's elbow. "Oh, no, not my Mary."

Edith and Percy Blyth, the church custodians, had assumed the role of Mary's godparents. They loved the girl as if she was their own. Only their son, Roger held such a place their hearts, and unfortunately, him livin' in St. Louis, they didn't get to see him near as often as they liked.

"Hold on now," Casey said, raising his hands to try and quell the growing clamor of the concerned gathering. "We don't know that anything is amiss just yet."

Turning back to Pastor Wilson he asked, "Have you spoken with Trace and Odette. Maybe the girls went straight there because of that tree bein' down up the way. Odette may have insisted that Mary spend the night rather than go back out in that storm."

"I checked with them when Mary didn't show,"

Wilson said, shaking his head. "Trace figured the kids must have overnighted with the Colby's. He said Tyrone wouldn't dare risk his horse by takin' it out in that storm. Since none of the party goers came back past my place, I figured he must be right."

Casey paled. "You, of course didn't know 'bout that downed tree," he said. "We had to go plumb 'round to Beckett Lane to get past it. We never came by your place. I'm sorry."

"Pa?" I said, at a total loss for words. I had me a holler in the pit of my stomach I guess Forrest Weston could o' played a game o' skittles in.

"Ain't no one's fault," Pa interjected as he stepped forward and squeezed Casey's shoulder. "And no time for second guessin'. What we gotta do is get out there and find them gals."

There was a general chorus of agreement from the crowd with utterances of, "That's right." — and, "If anyone can find them girls, Zeb can." — and, "Amen, brother."

With that, there was no need for debate. Pa was in charge.

"Casey, you head over and let Trace know what's

going on," he said. Then turning to Mr. Grear, "I'd appreciate it if you could drop Kathryn, Delma, and J.J. off at Forrest's place. Me and Billy'll be needin' Mac and Cornpone."

"Not a problem, Zeb," Mr. Grear said. "What else can I do for ya?"

"Gather some folks together to build a signal pyre. One here, and one atop Rich Mountain. Be sure to use enough green brush to make plenty o' smoke. Light em up if them girls show, to let the searchers know to come in. Don't want no one stumblin' around out there any longer than need be."

Lookin' over a few heads, he said, "Chance, we could use your dogs."

"You got it Zeb," Chance called. "Pastor, you got somethin' with Mary's scent on it?"

"Yeah, will a shawl do?" Wilson asked.

"That'll do fine," Chance acknowledged.

"I'll get with ya, after I drop my family off," Forrest told Chance. "We'll pick your boy up over at the Methodist Church on the way."

"I appreciate that," Chance said. "I know he'll wanna be there. That little Beckett gal's done got him

243

house broke, sittin' up straight, and rollin' over." He shook his head with a baleful grin. "Plumb painful to watch, if you ask me."

Forrest grinned. "Happens to the best of us," he chuckled, glancin' over his shoulder.

Casey saw the jest in his brother's eye, but let it ride. "Thelma," he said, "you go with Lidia. It might help if y'all check with everyone who came back with us. Maybe someone heard something we're not aware of."

"That's a good idea," said Pa.

He hadn't missed the dart flung between siblings either, but didn't feel now was the time for levity. He'd store it away for later.

Lookin' across the congregation, he said, "Anyone who's lookin' to join in the search, meet at the foot of Rich Mountain Road within the hour. Them girls could be in trouble and we ain't got time to waste."

"Church is dismissed," called Wilson. Then, with a slight tick twitching the sallow skin beneath his left eye, he looked at Pa and said, "I'll have my horse ready as soon as I get Brother Fieldman, Mary's shawl."

"No," said Pa, laying his big hand on the man's shoulder. "I'm afraid you've got the toughest job of all. You need to be here when Mary shows up. Could be she'll be needin' ya real bad. Ain't nobody can comfort a girl like her own Pa."

Wilson paled. He knew Pa was right. But waitin' in uncertainty was about the hardest thing a man could do.

"Okay, Zeb," he said. "If you think it's best."

I reckon Pa had it figured we'd be coverin' some mighty tough territory in a mighty big hurry. Pastor Wilson just wasn't up to the task. He was a sure enough fine fella, mind you. Just nobody's idea of a mountain man.

So, with a plan in motion, everyone split-up and got to the job at hand. And not a bit too soon either, to my way o' thinkin'.

≈

Diver and Charlotte sat up the rest of the night, coddlin' and fussin' over Pauline. Neither dared voice how similar her symptoms were to those of little

Dennis that first night of his sickness, but in all truth, there was no denyin' it.

The pitiful gasping for breath. The mucus clogged nostrils and persistent dry coughing. The clammy skin and wracking shivers. And, perhaps worst of all, the glistening dampness of dull weepy eyes lost in a daunting, far-away gaze.

It was downright heart-rending. And it was Dennis all over again.

Then, as the cock's first crow heralded the early morning sun, her symptoms eased. The weak, raspy breathing settled. Her puffy red eyelids drooped — then closed. Pauline slipped into an exhausted slumber. Unfortunately, these seemingly encouraging developments mimicked Dennis's ailment also.

The coming night would tell.

Foregoing church: unwilling to expose Pauline to the elements, and neither willing to be apart from her in her hour of need, they held their own prayer service there at home. Nestled close around her bassinet, they thanked their Lord for all the blessings He had bestowed upon them. For their friends and family, and the multitude of little miracles that enhanced their daily lives.

"And, please," Diver prayed, one hand holding Charlottes' and the other resting on Pauline's chest, "grant us a little more time with our precious child. With your wonderous gift."

Diver's heart seemed to seize in his chest as he ended with: "Thy will be done. Amen."

As time slipped away, long shafts of wavering sunbeams spilled though Charlotte's 'cylinder glass' windowpanes. Intricate patterns of varying hues, (distortions wrought by imperfections in the hand-blowing process), traced their way slowly across the pinewood floorboards. The cabin warmed. The night-chill lifted.

Outside, cottony mist began to drift toward the ridgetops. Long drooping branches, and flattened fields of over-grown wild grasses shed their sodden burdens and lifted their clinging foliage to the clear, blue, southern skies.

High up in a secluded mountain valley, a family of tawny whitetail deer nibbled their way along as they slipped through wavering tendrils of rising vapor. On occasion, the stealthy adults froze in place as the twin

247

yearlings bolted away, chasing each other through the thinning mist. Even with their overly cautious upbringing, they at times just couldn't resist letting loose and cavorting across the wide-open meadows. Especially on frosty mornings, when only their ears and the tip of their tails occasionally appeared above the low hanging clouds.

But then, nothing lasts forever.

As the sun crawled higher into the sky, burning off the haze, it exposed the meadows to spying eyes. Eyes to be avoided at all times. A lifetime of fleeing every type of danger the mountains had to offer had taught the wily ol' buck many lessons. Mastery of which was testified by his ripe old age of seven years. In the wild, mistakes seldom accord a second chance.

By the time the mist faded, he led his family deep into the safety of the thickets. He knew the shortening of daylight hours and the hint of frost carried on the breeze spurred animals of prey to fatten up in preparation of the cold times to come. Until the bitter chill of mid-winter prohibited easy nocturnal foraging, he'd alleviate daytime travel as much as possible.

By mid-morning the family of whitetails were comfortably nestled in an overgrown patch of cattail stalks deep in the backwoods. Their stomachs were full of acorns and flint corn, and they were ready to doze the heat of the day away.

But even as the mists cleared and game animals slunk away to protected alcoves, a whole different order of critters were emerging from their dens.

Nature's true workforce began poking their heads from deep rocky crags, mud-fringed borrows, and tightly woven twig and grass nests that swayed high in the treetops.

The builders, cleaners, and cultivators of the forest cared little about the whims of man or nature. The previous night's deluge was nothing more than a convenient supply of water. An up-rooted tree, raw material at hand. As for the trials and tribulations it may have caused to man; no thought at all.

The underlings, the ignored, the overlooked hordes of nature's renovators carried on as they had in perpetuity; mindlessly unaware and unconcerned about the frenzied citizenry of the Cove, or the fears faced by loving parents lamenting the trials of their infant daughter.

Fears that Diver and Charlotte valiantly tried to keep in check. Tried not to put too much emphasis on. Similarities between Pauline and Dennis's illnesses were not proof positive of doom.

After all, kids do occasionally get sick.

Trying to alleviate her fears by keeping busy, Charlotte prepared a light lunch of broiled mutton, mashed potatoes, and seared onions, along with stale cornbread and a pitcher of cold buttermilk.

Neither Diver nor herself having eaten breakfast, she hoped the comfort food would ease their minds as their daughter slept.

Just as Charlotte had concluded, "*a busy mind is a contented mind*," so had Diver. While Charlotte worked on the midday meal, he headed out to do something about that annoying fence board. He'd not given it much thought over the last few days, figuring he'd get to it eventually, but after the racket it caused last night; well, now was as good a time as any.

Standing there, hammer in hand, nails in mouth, he thought about Pauline sleeping mere feet away, inside the house. If that board could be as disruptive as it was, what would slamming an iron-headed hammer into a solid cedar plank sound like?

He was obviously gonna have to come up with a better plan.

After a moment's thought, he put his tools away and silently tied the loose board to the post.

"That'll do for now," he mumbled as he stood back and looked at his handy work.

And so, the day wore on. Each parent aimlessly diving into one labor after the next. Chore after chore. Task after task. Many that were days away from needing attention. Anything to take their minds off their deepest fears.

Finally, shortly after noon, they heard Pauline stir. With a jolt of adrenaline coursing through their veins, they hurried to her side.

She was awake! Other than a single tear that dampened the curly hairs just below her left ear, she looked on the mend. Refreshed. More lucid.

"Her eyes look clearer," Charlotte beamed as she stooped low and cooed at the child. Diver's heart swelled. He couldn't even speak. He simply nodded.

Gently picking up the baby, Charlotte sat on the

251

edge of the bed and fed her. It was without a doubt, with only limited success, but Pauline did receive a bit of nourishment.

Moments later, she happily blew baby bubbles before drifting back to sleep.

After carefully changing and bathing the child, Charlotte freshened up the bassinet and eased her down. The rest of the afternoon was one of guarded elation. Husband and wife, sitting hand in hand, laughing, and reminiscing. They even played a game of checkers.

Then, as an evening chill drifted across the floor, a raspy cough pierced their hearts.

FIFTEEN

Pixies

MARY SHIVERED AS SHE tugged on her filthy blankets. Try as she might, she couldn't alleviate a cold chill that had settled into the small of her back. That, along with a pebble the size of Hec Rucker's anvil digging at her left hip, made sleep as elusive as an overzealous tax collector on Sunday mornin'.

Of course, in all truth, she knew things could have been worse.

Letting her heart resettle after retrieving her 'haint blanket' from its lofty heights, she'd scrambled across shattered boulders beneath the cliff face to retrieve the other one. Between the two, she at least had a semblance of protection from the night's chill.

"I'm probably a sight better off than Susan is

anyway," she mumbled as she gave the blankets yet another tug. "Serve her right if all them fancy curls her ma put in her hair froze and snapped off in her sleep."

She slapped a hand over her mouth and chuckled at the thought. Susan scramblin' around, frantically pickin' up ice-incrusted curls and tryin' to stick 'em back on her half bald head.

Suddenly she realized how petty the thought was. How unkind. Not at all the way Pa had raised her.

But it sure was funny, she thought with a smile.

Staring at the heavens with sleepless eyes, she watched dark clusters of ragged clouds; obviously the remnants of bygone storms, trace their way across mournful sky. Lofty apparitions, like great celestial ships of war, they jostled for position before crashing one upon the other to form a chaotic mass of mangled peril. Then, as if by design, scattered once again to continue their never-ending voyage across the cosmos. Aloof and unconcerned with consequences incurred by their futile battles, they at times blotted out the waning moon, and at others, let it shine. In so doing, they created an altercation of lunar brilliance that wavered across a nearby cliff face with varying hues.

Mary, aghast and awestruck, couldn't help but notice the rocky craig as it fluctuated between light and dark. Clustered shadows creeping across the stony precipice transformed pitted hollows and ageless cracks into sunken cheeks, glaring eyes, and the hard, straight lips of a very unhappy woman.

An Indian woman. A stone-faced witch.

And the witch was staring straight at her.

"Eek!" Mary squealed as a gentle breeze delicately brushed a drooping blade of bluestem grass across the curve of her right ear. Unseen in the murky darkness, her heart nearly exploded as she viciously slapped at the offending presence. In her startled state of mind, it could be nothing short of an attacking minion sent forth by the stone-faced witch. A messenger of death and doom who would once and for all rid these hidden prominences and shadowy dales from the bungling antics of this meager mortal girl.

Too frightened to stand on reason, Mary gave in to a sudden fit of panic. Swatting and jabbing, she tried in vain to drive the perceived phantom away. But

255

with every sweep of her hand, it simply fluttered back, then returned with its prickly point.

Unfortunately, as the fray continued, the sharp tip flicked about; nicking and slashing, causing thin rivulets of blood to soon appear. Stinging welts began to rise across her cheeks and bare neck. The more she struggled, the more she was convinced she was under attack.

Screeching in desperation, she reached back with both open hands and like a giant crab on the seashore, clamped her fingers around the offending stem. Then, roaring in rage, and blinded by terror, she ripped the entire clump of greenery from the rocky soil.

Dirt flew, rocks clattered. Mary, panting with fright, sat in the dark staring at the creature held captive in her hands. A creature that had ceased to be a threat. But what was it? Never had she seen such a strange apparition.

It was then that the moon peeked between the clouds and illuminated the scene. To her amazement, the mysterious beast transformed into nothing more than a clump of common, little bluestem grass. The same grass that flourished along the shoulder of

Baptist Church Road back home. A grass she'd been familiar with her whole life.

She opened her hands and let the innocuous debris fall to the ground. What could it possibly mean?

Looking back up at the barren cliff, the moon having advanced slightly in the sky, nothing remained of the apparition except rocky slabs, shadowy cracks, and jagged crevices. The figure had vanished. Melded back into the stone. The vengeful witch was gone. All that remained was a quickly fleeting illusion brought on by an overwrought imagination.

Mary laughed.

"So much for never fearing a chestnut haint again," she muttered.

Then, as if to stifle her reprieve, a haunting sound beckoned on the breeze.

"Arreee ... Arrreee!"

Drifting through the treetops, echoing off the craggy bluff face, the high-pitched, warbling cry froze Mary to the core. It was as if the stone-faced witch had flowed down off the precipice and settled into her mortal soul.

Mary quickly scrambled deep into the crevice beneath an overhanging boulder. Pulling her blankets in after herself, she wadded them into a tangled ball and clamped them tightly over her head and face to stifle a heart-wrenching shriek. Even the stench and filth of the harshly used linens was better than facing the terrors on the wind.

Would this night never end?

Clinching her teeth, she squeezed her eyes shut. Her chest ached from the persistent pounding of her heart. Her throat spasmed from the half-restrained scream. Her mind reeled with tormenting thoughts of, "All hope lost!"

Mercifully, long before daybreak, Mary fell into an exhausted, and much needed slumber.

Dappled light filtered through the autumn canopy that shaded Mary's grotto. The soft burble of a nearby stream gently serenaded the woodland denizens, enticing them to partake in a few extra luxurious moments of glorious, soul soothing sleep. To extend their much-needed reprieve before crawling out to face the harsh dealings of another day.

But not everyone seemed to have received the message.

Suddenly, as if bellowing a call to arms, the neighborhood nuisance, a boisterous, leaf imitating katydid, let loose with a loud, staccato-like chirp, sounding astonishingly like the insect version of a billy goat's bleat.

Mary opened her eyes.

Amazingly, what laid before her was a virtual wonderland to the senses. A dazzling spectacle as if ripped from the pages of her childhood dreams.

Shimmering glints of clustered pyrite incrusted with mica and quartzite chips sparkled across the patch of rock-strewn ground that stretched out before her. Dazzling flickers of white, red, and blue twinkled in the sunlight, dancing to the melody of the gently flowing stream.

As if not to be outdone, a plethora of long, thin, strands of silky spider's gossamer glistened as they floated by, carried on the morning breeze. They twirled and twisted, and occasionally got caught on delicate pine needles or seed-bearing cones where they were left flapping in the wind like beautiful, discarded, bridal veils.

"Pixie veils!" Mary whispered. "The last vestiges of the most elusive brides in the fairy realm."

Willingly giving into her childhood fantasies, Mary pictured the pixies flittering away at the first twinkling of her eyelids opening. Disappearing in such a hurry they even left their precious veils behind.

As for the katydid? He was obviously a guest of honor, Mary mused.

Perhaps his bleating chirp has come down through the ages as a sought-after wedding ditty. A song that placed him in favor with the bride. But unfortunately, not being blessed with the pixie's heightened senses and rapid reflexes, he seemed to have been caught unawares by the sudden departure of the wedding party. And the attendees also.

The dim-witted katydid sat there all alone; clueless and wondering where everyone had gone.

Suddenly, as if to add insult to injury, an orange and black beetle, fluttered down and landed on his bulbous, emerald wings.

The katydid froze.

Gently folding its flexible hind wings in place, the beetle settled its hardened forewings over them and prepared for lunch. Selecting what looked to be a tasty morsel of tender leaf, he extended his sharp-tipped mandibles and dug in.

As you might imagine, like most folks, katydids don't much care to be nibbled on.

In a flurry of pumping legs, flailing wings, and flicking antenna, the katydid shook off the startled beetle and burst into flight. Achieving what must have been a record-breaking pace for the notoriously poor flying species, he flittered across the flowing stream and quickly took shelter deep within a thick clump of half-dead Indian grass.

"I feel for ya, little fella," Mary chuckled as she watched the miniature drama unfold before her. "Attend a wedding in your finest suit and get taken for a tasty milkweed."

A smile crossed her lips.

How absolutely delightful … and bewildering, she thought. I passed out in the darkened clutches of pain and terror and awoke among the silvery glow of a mountain fairyland. Even missed out on witnessing a clandestine pixie wedding by no more than the twinkle of a moment.

Mary laid back and stretching out her arms yawned. She then placed her hands behind her head and closed her eyes.

"Maybe I'll curl up and get a bit more sleep," she muttered to herself.

Suddenly, a long gurgling rumble echoed through the alcove. A sound that Mary had often asked the Lord to never let happen while in church services.

Grabbing her protesting stomach, Mary giggled and said, "Well, perhaps not."

Gathering up her dirty blankets, she crawled out of the dusty hole where she'd sheltered for the night. It certainly wasn't an abode she'd be hankerin' to move into on a permanent basis, but she was grateful for it all the same. After all, the humblest of hovels when times are fair become sheltering mansions in the face of despair.

As she stood with the fairy-patch sparkling like glitter about her feet, she couldn't help but thrill in the majesty of the place. The beauty. The serenity.

A calmness settled over her.

The skies above were clear, the clouds swept away. A warm breeze was blowing in from the south. The kind of warmth that, caressing the skin like a mother's tender hug leaves a tingling sheen of moisture glistening on your upper lip. The kind of warmth Mary never thought she'd feel again.

The gossamer strands, (pixie veils, if you will), caught in the breeze and carried on high, twinkled in the sun as they drifted away. Mary's heart soared with the delicate silk as if riding the cosmos with them.

In that moment, anything seemed possible. Even finding her way home. And when she did, she knew she'd be taking a piece of that enchanted realm with her.

Well, I'm here to tell ya, that's just what she done. Yes sir, I was witness to it. Fact is, it sometimes gets me all croupy throated and misty-eyed just at the rememberin' of it. Ya see, every now and then ... 'specially durin' them long dog days of autumn, Mary would seem to kinda drift away while sittin' there knittin' on my Bible socks. (Them's the holey ones.) Or maybe she'd go to missin' the bowl while poppin' snap beans, slowly rockin' on Ma's ol' porch chair.

Whatever the case may be, when I saw them things happenin', I'd get all nervous and jittery, wonderin' what the problem might be. Then I'd notice that long away look in her big, beautiful, glistening eyes, and I'd know she'd once again journeyed away to some far-off wilderness fairyland. Her personal retreat of peace and safety. A place tucked away so deeply in the recesses of her mind that not even I could journey there with her.

Not that I begrudged her the respite. No one deserved a moment of tranquility more than Mary did.

Then, as I'd sit there, lookin' in complete awe at God's finest creation restin' right there on my front porch, the most serene look of contentment would wash over her face. I'm talkin' the look of pure joy.

As I live, it was a site to behold. A site I'll treasure to the end of my days. I reckon ya might laugh at the notion, but lookin' back at it now, I think she glowed.

You know, I never did ask, but from the smile on her face, I wouldn't be at all surprised if them pixies didn't come on back and invite her to join in on the weddin' festivities.

Now ain't that somethin'?

Course, I can't say if it's so or not, but I'll tell ya this, it sure tickles me to think it is.

Anyway, after Mary crawled from the hovel, she went down to the stream and found a swift moving riffle where she could get herself a drink. A clear flowing spring would have been preferable, but with none in view the quick moving rapids were at least better than slow, silty backwater pools.

As she quenched her parched throat, a fluttering of yellow, black, and white caught her attention from a short distance downstream. Sitting up and shielding her eyes from the early morning sun, she watched as two twittering goldfinches darted about, plucking seeds from a shaded stand of cattails.

Mary smiled. She'd often heard that if your ever lost in the wilderness and need something to eat, just keep an eye out for God's creatures. The forest is their dinner table. To be sure, you can't eat everything they do, but they'll likely lead you to something you can.

It's better than hopin' to stumble across goats, grain and raisins like old Robinson Crusoe did in that book by Daniel Defoe, Mary figured. Not that she could cook a goat even if she did catch one.

And Mary wasn't about to start grazin' in the fields like ol' Nebuchadnezzar did either.

As it just so happened, last year, on their way to Trenton, New Jersey to settle her grandfather's affairs, Mary and her father had stopped to eat lunch near a small, cattail bordered pond. Not one to miss out on a learning opportunity, her pa had proceeded to tell her how nearly every part of the semi-aquatic plant was edible. Then, being a believer that demonstration is a better educator than elucidation, he muddied his boots, and nearly took an unexpected dip in the cold murky waters trying to pull one of the stubborn, cotton-headed weeds from the mire.

After finally procuring his prize, he happily trudged back up the embankment.

Mary remembered how she held back a snicker when he stopped to rake his soiled boots through a deadly patch of horse nettle. He looked just like Lucy Stover's little brother that time he stepped on a fresh cow patty. They'd both kicked and wiped and stomped about, not accomplishing much of anything other than spreadin' the muck halfway up their pant legs before giving up.

"Now, if ya look here," her pa said as he held out the tall, wild vegetable. "These long leaves are good for weaving mats and baskets and are even edible when they're young and tender." Then, digging a thumbnail into a vein on the leaf, he showed her a white viscous liquid. "The sap is known to soothe toothaches, headaches, and help heal wounds."

Turning the plant upright, he said, "This brown head makes a tolerable torch when you dip it in oil or fat, and since its water-tight in the heaviest rains, it can be shredded and used as a fire starter."

He pulled out a pinch of fluff and held it up. "It even has nutty tasting seeds in it, though I gotta admit, they are mighty small."

Trying to demonstrate how to nibble on the miniature pods, he wound up in a spitting fit as he aggressively wiped at his tongue. Looking up with a timid smile, he had tiny strands of fluff clinging to his lips and the whiskers of his chin.

Undaunted, he continued. "When the head is young and green, it can be eaten raw or cooked like corn on the cob. I've heard it said it resembles mashed potatoes. You can also collect the pollen from the upper, male, flower head, or dry and crush the roots to make a decent flour."

He ripped off the leaves. "But this time of year, the best parts of the plant are its roots, and lower shoots."

Snapping the stalk off several inches above the base, he pulled off the outer sheafs like peeling an onion. Inside, the snowy-white core of the plant was soon revealed. "This is my favorite part," he said.

Placing the half-inch thick stem in his mouth, he bit a piece off and began chewing. After a moment he drew a small, stiff, sliver from between his lips and flicked it away. "Not bad," he quipped. Then offering the wild veggie to Mary, he said, "Here, try it."

A bit hesitantly, Mary placed the slightly sticky shoot between her teeth and snapped off a morsel like nibbling on a half-cooked section of string bean.

Immediately, a somewhat bitter, though quite mild essence of cucumber flooded her mouth. Her first reaction was to grimace, but the experience of witnessing a new flavor soon became intriguing.

"Kind of an acquired taste," her pa chuckled with

a grin on his face, "but it's completely safe, and quite nutritious, I assure you."

From that day forward, Mary marveled at the bounty God bestowed on mankind if he only had the wisdom to use it. As for herself, she didn't have a great deal of knowledge, but she did have an entire cattail patch to ease her hunger pangs. Over the next hour or so, she ate her fill before weaving a functional cattail basket for carrying extra shoots and roots along with her. Not knowing when she'd come across another patch, she wasn't taking any chances.

Afterwards, the day being uncommonly warm, she squealed and giggled as she sat on a flat stone in the middle of the frigid stream and washed the filth from her hair, and body. With skin rippling in goosebumps and redder than the leaves of late season sugar maples, she even chewed the tip of a hickory twig to a frazzle and used it for a toothbrush.

Just the simple act of being clean filled her with optimism. She might make it through this ordeal after all.

Then her eyes fell on the tattered, grime covered blankets. "What am I gonna do with you?" she asked.

Washing the cumbersome pieces of cloth wasn't an option. Warm day or not, they'd never dry before dark. And luggin' the sodden weight around all day was unthinkable anyway.

"Well, guess there's only one thing for it," she mumbled. Hanging the sheets over a limb, she found a good, heavy switch and walloped the tar out of em.

Forty minutes later, arm weary and sun-dried, Mary stood gasping at her reasonably dirt-free blankets.

"Better than wallerin' in filth like a momma sow," she mumbled.

By quarter to noon, she was back on the trail.

SIXTEEN

Calm Water

CHARLOTTE WIPED TEARS FROM her eyes as Diver once again placed Pauline face down on his out-stretched arm. Just as he had the previous night, he rested her swollen neck between the widely spread fingers of his left hand and slightly tilted her head toward the floor.

The child gagged and squirmed as she gasped for breath. Dank strands of disheveled, golden hair laid plastered to the side of her face. Tiny, blue hued veins bulged from her neck.

Gently rubbing and patting her sweaty back, he jostled his arm up and down as a yellow-grey mucus expelled from her airways. Phlegm dribbled down and splattered the bare-wood floor between his feet.

Suddenly, Pauline retched. Lumpy, viscous liquid

spewed across Diver's right legs and collected on his leather shoes. She then sucked in a quick gasp of life-giving air and loosed a shrill, heart-wrenching wail.

Charlotte clasped her hands tightly before her breast and let out a long-pent-up breath as tears rolled down her face.

Diver raised Pauline up and rested her head on his shoulder. Drool seeped from her mouth and clotted specks clung to her cheeks, nose, and chin. In Diver's mind, she had never looked more beautiful.

Suddenly, her bowels shifted, and a pungent odor permeated the room. Charlotte couldn't help but laugh at the spontaneous reaction that distorted Diver's face. His eyes squinted; his nose wrinkled; and he pulled his chin back over his right shoulder.

Charlotte reached out and took the child. Even so, she marveled at the wisdom of the man.

Long years of treating young Dennis for a mysterious bronchial ailment had taught Diver how to handle emergency bouts of congestive suffering. Time and again, he had pulled Dennis through agonizing fits of choking and coughing using the same method he had just plied to Pauline. Born of desperation, and acknowledged as temporary at best, it was at least more useful than the well-intended ministrations of woefully inadequate, Kentucky doctors, who sorrowfully asserted that nothing could be done.

After clearing Dennis's airway, and gently massaging his back until normal breathing returned, Diver and Charlotte had remained near his bedside for hours, until convinced the crisis had been averted.

Not willing to except the futility of fighting the ailment, Diver had read about and spoken with anyone who had the slightest knowledge of the condition. He'd discovered that after an attack, dry smokeless heat in the winter, and lots of fresh air in the summer, seemed to be the best treatment available. That, along with any number of warm herbal teas that helped to open the passageways and break up the mucus.

As for preventing an attack in the first place, he learned that as the boy aged, plenty of exercise to strengthen the body and long walks to build up stamina, seemed to be the ticket.

But alas, even with constant vigilance and patient care, Diver had only managed to postpone the inevitable. Dennis lost the battle when exposed to a flu epidemic in his fifteenth year.

Only God knew how Charlotte and Diver could possibly survive if the worst happened again. And Charlotte not only had to contend with the threat of losing another child; the last child she would ever have if the doctors were correct, but also with the fear that the heartbreak could take her husband as well.

After cleaning up and changing Pauline, Charlotte wrapped her in a soft blanket and sat at the kitchen table spoon-feeding her small sips of warm ginger-and-honey tea.

They had discovered with Dennis that ginger-and-honey seemed to be the most effective remedy for breaking up mucus and restoring breathing.

Pauline's breathing *had* improved, but she still remained lethargic.

"You think Doc Dulaney could help?" Charlotte asked as she used the tip of the spoon to capture an errant dribble off of Pauline's chin.

Diver considered that a while as he aimlessly paced around the kitchen table. He'd not had much luck with the doctors back home, and he certainly wouldn't wish Doc Kendree on his worst enemy, but that didn't mean he disregarded the entire profession as a matter of course.

"He seems to be a smart young fella," he said. "And fresh out of college too."

He leaned over and listened to Pauline's breathing.

"Outta know the latest practices and theories."

There was a slight wheezing, but nothing like it had been earlier.

"Wouldn't hurt none to see what he has to say."

Pauline's eyes drooped shut and moments later her breathing evened out. The ordeal had been taxing and her tiny body needed rest.

Charlotte quietly laid the spoon on the table, then gently eased a single strand of silky hair away from the corner of the child's mouth. Tears gathered on her eyelashes. She quickly wiped them away before they fell on Pauline's face.

"Get him," Charlotte said in a voice so low, Diver had to contemplate on it before the words sank in.

Retrieving his hat and jacket from their hanger pegs, he laid them across his left arm before easing the front door open and slipping outside. He then donned his outerwear as he hurried across the yard to his three-stall stable and tack shed.

Aristotle saw him coming from where he stood munching a tender clump of timothy grass near the far fencerow. With a nicker and a shake of his head, he bolted across the pasture to greet his master.

"Yeah, come on boy," Diver called as he unlatched the gate and headed for the tack shed. "We got work to do."

In less than five minutes, Diver and Aristotle were at full gallop, rounding the bend onto Baptist Church Road.

Mary trudged through unfamiliar woodlands all day. She had no idea where she was headed but figured since people settled on waterways, she'd have to come across someone eventually. After all, every child of the mountains knew how Mary Draper Ingles had found her way home after escaping a Shawnee village by following the river.

She'd nibbled on her cattail hearts, an occasional

wild onion, and more persimmons than she cared to think about. Wrapped in her blankets, she carried a substantial supply of chestnuts; husk and all. She figured huskin', shellin', and diggin' out the meat, would be a good job for when she had settled in for the night. It would certainly be a more pleasant task than trying to hide from hickory haints or bluff sized witchy women.

As the autumn sun settled among towering distant hills, a cold breeze kicked up causing long sweeping ripples to race across a section of slow-movin' stream. Tiny fish, perceiving the movement, darted about hoping to capture any unfortunate, tasty insects that may have been dislodged from the foliage above. As they spattered the mirrored surface with a thousand concentric circles, gloomy shadows drifted across the landscape. Both in water and out, what had been crystal clear objects, transformed to murky, indistinguishable, and mysterious forms.

Time was gettin' short. After a long day of tirelessly stomping through a seemingly endless patch of mountain laurel, and forever winding her way around tangled masses of discarded river debris, she desperately needed to find a suitable refuge, a shelter for the night. Her feet felt as though they were chiseled from granite fieldstones, and every step she took forced her to find the fortitude to take another. Never in her life had she felt so exhausted.

Stopping to catch her breath, blankets tucked under her left arm, she clasped her long tattered skirt in her right hand to keep it from snagging on sharp thorny thickets. She studied a white-faced cliff in the gathering gloam.

Looks like a cavity under that rocky shelf, she thought. Could be home for the night.

Pulling at her long skirt once again – ripping a five-inch strip of cloth from her petticoat in the process, she scrambled over a fallen log and made her way across a narrow floodplain to the base of the declivity.

It was about five feet above the valley floor, and from what she could see, dark and dingy. At perhaps twelve-feet long, four-feet high, and eight-feet deep, it didn't look to be the most secure of abodes she could have imagined, but it'd keep her out of inclement weather all the same.

Taking hold of her blankets with both hands, she tossed them onto the self.

A blue-tailed lizard burst from the opening and scurried across the ledge, disappearing into a narrow fissure. Almost immediately, he reappeared several inches further down the crack and leapt into a patch of gamagrass where he paused a moment; swaying on a long glossy blade. Its brown and white striped ribcage rose and fell as the tip of its tongue slightly protruded from its tan-rimmed mouth. It eyed Mary as it stood stock still; one long fingered hand raised high in preparation of fleeing if need be.

"Sorry little fella," Mary said with a grin. "Didn't mean to kick ya outta your house. But I reckon I need it more than you do."

The lizard flicked its tail and vanished into the scrub.

"See ya," called Mary.

Looking over a nearby fallen tree, she found a stout looking limb she was able snap off. Dragging it back to the rocky recess, she stood on tiptoes as she wildly jabbed and thrashed it about. In no time she'd raked every declivity and crevice she could reach, ridding them of any potential squiggling, scampering or hissing roommates she might encounter. Dust billowed, and small rocks clattered off the walls. Her blankets shifted, spilling chestnuts across the floor. But to Mary's relief, no additional critters made an appearance.

"I reckon that'll do it," she said to herself as she searched for a good toe hold to help her clammer into the hollow. Finding one, she clasped a bumpy nodule with her right hand and the self-lip with her left.

"Umph," she groaned as she started to scale the five-foot facade.

"Aarrry!"

She kicked away and dropped to the forest floor. Spinning around, she thrust both hands out in front of herself to ward off the haunting refrain. It was the same sound she'd heard the night before. Had the Indian witch followed her all the way here?

"Marrry!"

There it was again.

"Marrryyy!"

Looking slightly to her right, she saw movement. It was on the far side of the stream. It looked like a giant bird flapping its wings.

"Oh, Mary. Is it really you?"

As her eyes began to focus, and the clump of terror eased in her throat, the mysterious bird began to meld. Its wings became arms, and its screeching beak, a face.

Could it be?

Mary stared dumbfounded into the gloom.

Susan?

"Susan is that you?" she called.

"Oh, Mary," cried Susan, with a trimmer in her voice. "I've been so scared."

Mary hurried across the floodplain to the darkening, slow-moving, watercourse. She could see Susan standing on the far bank, grasping an under-washed sapling.

"How did you get here?" she called.

"I followed the river," Susan called back.

"But how did you get..." Mary indicated the water, "over there?"

"I don't know," Susan whined, "but I'm coming to you."

It immediately registered to Mary that calm water

is deep water. Her Pa had taught her that.

"No, Susan! Don't ..." she shouted as a resounding 'kerplunk' filled the twilight.

Susan, trying to use the sapling to ease her way down to the water, landed rump first in the frigid stream when the embankment gave way. A moment later she resurfaced ten feet from shore. Slapping and splashing, too shocked to vocalize, she managed no more than a 'yelp' before going under again.

Mary knew Susan swam like a nine-pound hammer. Quickly yanking her bulky dress over her head, she threw it aside and leapt into the icy depths.

The shock was more than she'd anticipated.

With her breath ripped from her chest, and her tender flesh sizzling like a pork chop fryin' in bear fat, she imagined for a terrifying moment that her and Susan were both gonna drown.

It was a slap in the face and a vicious tug of her hair that brought her back to reality. Somehow, she and Susan had found each other in mid-stream. And Susan, panicked as she was, was in the process of tryin' to climb on top of her head.

"Quit!" gasped Mary, swallowing a lung searing

mouth-full of ice-cold water. "Quit ... agh," she went under, then resurfaced. "I said..."

By this time Susan had one leg thrust over Mary's shoulder and was trying to climb her like a stepladder.

Desperately gulping for air, Mary reached up behind Susan's back and grabbed a handful of her curly hair. Calling on every last ounce of energy that she had, she pulled.

"Eek ... splu..." Susan lost her grip and cartwheeled into the stream backwards.

Without releasing her hand-full of clammy tresses, Mary kicked for the shore.

"Wha ... you ... drown me," Susan gasped as her face broke the surface.

By then, Mary's feet had found purchase. She fell back against the bank and drug Susan's struggling form after her.

Susan continued to clasp and grab at Mary, spittin' and sputtering as if she was still in mid-stream.

"Quit it! Quit it," screamed Mary.

Susan continued to struggle.

"I said stop!" bellowed Mary. She reached back

and slapped the girl across her cheek.

Susan froze, eyes as big as October puffballs. She stared at Mary like the puppy who got scolded when the cat turned over the sugar bowl.

"Your safe now," Mary said. "You can quit strugglin'."

Tears began streaming down Susan's cheeks. "Why are you so mean to me?" she blubbered. "I just wanted to be with you."

"Mean to you?" blared Mary. "You were tryin' to drown me."

Susan covered her face with muddy hands and began to cry in earnest.

"What?" Mary blurted. She couldn't believe she was actually feeling that she was in the wrong. The girl *had* tried to drown her.

"The fact is, none of this would have happened in the first place if you hadn't run off with the horse and left me to be eaten by those wild coyotes," she spewed.

Susan stopped crying and looked up.

"What horse?" she asked.

"Tyrone's horse," Mary blurted.

Susan shook her head. "I didn't take the horse. In

fact, I didn't even think about the horse. I was so scared when I got out of that hole, I just ran. I ran as far, and as fast, as I could. I was so sure them beasts were gonna get me, I guess I panicked. By the time I came to my senses, I didn't know where I was, or where you were. I called for you, but you didn't answer. I've called for you ever since."

Mary was flabbergasted. If Susan hadn't taken the horse, who had? Then it stuck her. Of course, Susan hadn't taken the horse. If the horse had been there when the coyotes arrived, they would have eaten it. It must have broken loose when it first smelled em comin'. Here she'd been wrongly blaming Susan all along.

"I'm sorry I ran off without ya though," said Susan.

Mary laid her hand on the shivering girls back. "No reason to be sorry," she said. "If I'd a got out first, I'd a done the same thing." She then pulled Susan close and hugged her. Susan rather doubted that Mary would have left her but didn't say anything.

Mary picked up her dress and turned toward the alcove. "We better get wrapped in our blankets before we catch our death of cold," she said.

"Blankets!" pealed Susan. "You've got the blankets?"

"Yes," said Mary. "They're in a crevice in that cliff over yonder."

"Oh, Mary, I've been so cold," whimpered Susan.

A flash of guilt clouded Mary's conscience. She remembered thinking how it served Susan right to be stuck out there alone, without her blanket. She'd been so wrong.

"Well, you got one now," she said.

Ten minutes later they were both wrapped up tight, sleeping like they hadn't a care in the world. Not knowin' what tomorrow would bring.

SEVENTEEN

Discoveries, Fair and Foul

D OC DULANEY HEARD RAPIDLY approaching hoofbeats clatter up the roadway and stop short outside his front gate.

As of a few weeks past, visitors would have ridden right on into the yard and up to the porch itself. That's back before Ollie Kilpatrick put up a picket fence in lieu of payment for Doc takin' care of his ailin' grandmother.

Unfortunately, the old lady passed away in the end anyway, but Ollie claimed the comfortin' Doc gave her was "More'n a body could expect, and all that a Christian man could ask for."

Casting heavy-lidded eyes across the kitchen table, Doc returned his slightly used spoon to its place beside his soup bowl and dabbed his lips with a flax

287

linen napkin.

"Now, who could that be?" his wife, Hailee, wondered.

Having only recently returned after a long day of obligatory house-calls and wellness checks, he'd just settled in to enjoy a hot meal of pulled squirrel and chanterelle mushrooms smothered in a spicy buttermilk gravy sauce.

Ever since he'd treated young Robby Lindsey over in Hickory Flats for that stingin' catfish injury, the boy'd seen to it that he never ran shy of tree-rats again. Some folks claimed Robby just couldn't miss with that Sheperd's sling of his. Fortunately, Doc figured fox squirrel was about the finest eatin' critter God ever made, so he was tickled pink with every one he received.

That's what made it all the more disheartening when the commotion was heard out front.

Sittin' his coffee mug aside and poppin' a thumb-sized chunk of corn muffin into his mouth, he eased his weary bones off the woven seat of his favorite Shaker chair. Then, strollin' through the living room, he looked out the front window.

"Why, its Diver McCoy!" he called to his wife as he dropped the curtain back in place.

Goin' out front, he stretched out his right arm and leaned against a weathered post that supported the mossy overhang of his porch roof. Water trickled from the eaves: testament to a short-lived shower that had passed through earlier that evening. As he deeply inhaled the crisp, clean air, he sucked on a stringy morsel lodged between his two front teeth. Failing in the effort, he absentmindedly used a thumbnail to pry the nuisance loose.

The front door squeaked. Hailee appeared at his side wordlessly placing her arm around his waist.

Diver finished tetherin' Aristotle to a picket and unlatched the front gate.

"What can we do ya for?" Dulaney called as Diver hurried up the path.

Diver doffed his hat. "It's Pauline," he said. "She's ailin' somethin' fierce. I was hopin' ya might come by and take a look at her."

"Yeah, I can do that," said Dulaney. "What seems to be the problem?"

"Breathin' trouble," said Diver. "Got me and

Charlotte mighty concerned. That's how we lost our first born."

Hailee moaned and clutched her hand to her throat. Havin' a young'un of her own, she couldn't imagine living through such a loss.

"You head on back and comfort Charlotte," Dulaney said. "I'll be right behind ya."

"I appreciate it," said Diver. He then turned and hurried back toward Aristotle.

Rushing into the house, the doc shoveled a couple more spoonsful of supper down his gullet. He then gulped his lukewarm coffee. That looked to be all the nourishment he was gonna get for some time to come.

Truth be told, bein' the only doc that side of Sevierville, goin' without was more common than havin' plenty.

Grabbin' his hat, coat, and medical bag, he gave his wife a quick peck on the lips, then started to turn toward the back door.

"Hold up a second," she said, stuffin' a couple corn muffins into his coat pocket. "You be careful out there." She then rose on tiptoes to give him a bit more substantial nibble, when...

"Waaah!"

Hailee cringed as she glanced at the bedroom.

"Sounds like I got a young'un to see to myself," she said. Grabbing a clean dish towel, she flipped it over her shoulder. "Now, try not to be out too late. You look like you could use a week's sleep." She turned toward the bedroom, and her squalling child. "And button up your coat. It's gettin' cold out there."

"Yes dear," Dulaney chuckled. "I'll be home as soon as possible."

Haillee waved over her shoulder without lookin' back.

Shaking his head, Dulaney let the door clack shut behind him as he headed for the stable. From the sound of it, his boy, Toby was breathin' just fine.

Mary opened her eyes to find the blue-tailed lizard hangin' upside down on the rocky surface above her face. He tensed, and pulled up a bit tighter to the ceiling when he noticed her watchin' him.

"Well, what do you expect," she whispered. "Come into a girl's bedroom uninvited."

Not wantin' to disturb Susan's sleep, she purposely kept her voice low.

"Serve ya right if I gobbled ya down with a dash o' salt and a glass of green apple cider."

A mumbled voice emanated from the tangle of Susan's blanket. "You got green apple cider?"

"No, I don't have green apple cider," Mary chuckled.

The lizard took the opportunity to streak across the ceiling and vanish over the ledge, unequivocally omitting reptile from the menu.

"I thought you were asleep," said Mary.

"I *was* asleep until you started talkin' to ...?" Suddenly Susan's head popped out from under the blanket, her hands clutching the dusty fabric tight up under her chin. "Who *were* you talkin' to?"

Mary laughed. "Nobody," she said.

"I heard you talking to somebody," Susan insisted.

Mary shook her head. "It was a lizard."

Susan sat up and stared Mary in the eyes. "You were talking to a lizard?" she scoffed.

"Yes, I was talking to a lizard," Mary quipped.

"Seems I've been talking to a lot of strange things lately." She threw back her blanket and propped herself up on one elbow. "We got cattail hearts and chestnuts for breakfast. You hungry?"

Susan stared at her best friend as if she'd claimed to be on first name basis with the lizard King. Then, her belly rumbled. She couldn't help but grin.

"Yeah, I'm hungry," she said.

Both girls laughed and commenced to crackin' the meat out of chestnuts and nibblin' on cattail hearts. It was a bit like snackin' on bittersweet potatoes and under-ripe cucumbers, but after what they'd been through, couldn't have tasted better had it been turkey and gravy on a bed of pumpkin pie.

Finally, being satiated, they gathered their blankets, hopped from the ledge, and strolled to the stream for a long drink of cold water.

"After last night, I never thought I'd want another drop of water out of this river again," said Susan.

Mary grinned. "I can understand that," she said.

Susan bowed her head. "I *am* sorry."

Mary was a bit taken aback. It wasn't in Susan's nature to apologize. Ever!

"Don't worry about it," she said. "If I couldn't swim, I'd have done the same thing."

Susan looked up at her. "No," she murmured, "I don't believe you would have."

Mary bent down and hugged her. "Let's be on our way," she said. "I don't know where we're goin', but we'll go there together."

"Come on in," Diver called in a soft voice when Doc Dulaney tapped on the front door.

Wiping his feet on a woven reed doormat before entering the tidy clapboard dwelling, the doctor saw Diver and Charlotte sitting face to face on ladder back chairs. They had little Pauline cradled on their knees between them.

"She's burnin' up, Doc," Diver said as he acknowledged Dulaney. "A little bit ago she threw up, and now she can't seem to catch her breath. Our boy, Dennis was the same way, but he would wheeze; she's gasping."

Dulaney sat his bag on the floor and dropped his coat and hat in a corner. He then hurried over and knelt down next to Pauline. The first thing he noticed was a light blue tinge to her lips and around her eyes. He placed the back of his fingers against her cheek.

She was hot, sweaty, and shivering.

Gently pullin' back the blanket, he next examined her fingernails and feet.

"Uh-huh," he muttered.

Placing the palms of his hands beneath her head, he softly probed the sides of her throat with his thumbs. He nodded, then raised her drooping eyelids to check for clarity.

"Hmm," he sighed. He plucked a strand of damp hair from the corner of her mouth.

"What do ya think, Doc?" Diver implored. Deep creases of concern etching his forehead. "Think it might be what Dennis had?"

Charlotte released a strangled sob.

"He'd improve with the heat of summer each year, but come winter, congest up again."

Diver squeezed Charlotte's hand.

"He put up a good fight," A tear rolled down his cheek. "but when he was fifteen the flue spread through our community. He caught it. Wasn't nothin' we could do after that. He worsened and passed away within days."

Dulaney folded back the baby blanket once again and lowered his ear to Pauline's chest. She whimpered and sneezed in his hair, but he didn't seem to notice.

"Mm-hmm," he uttered.

After a bit he carefully turned her over and listened to her back. With a nearly imperceptible nod of his head, he said, "I definitely hear a crackle in there."

Then, reaching for the blanket, he rewrapped her and placed her on his shoulder. Patting her back with a cuffed hand, he listened as her dry cough became more productive.

"What do ya think?" questioned Diver.

"Well, it sounds to me like Dennis had what was long referred to as 'mucus catarrh'. In 1808 Rev. Charles Badham more accurately renamed it, 'bronchitis'".

"Yeah, that's what we thought," said Diver. "But my understanding is that bronchitis is rarely fatal."

"That's true," said Dulaney, "for most bronchitis'. But it's now believed that there are at least three forms of the disease. The most common is short to mid-term and is usually tolerated well. Another type can be sporadic — giving the patient time to heal between bouts. That one is more dangerous in old age. But the third — chronic bronchitis — is usually seasonal. For reasons we don't understand that one causes accumulative damage with each reoccurrence. It wears the body down beyond its ability to continue the fight. Some patients outlast it, but many, usually due to an outside influence — as in Dennis' case, the flue — succumb.

"And Pauline?" asked Charlotte.

Dulaney rubbed the child's back, then placed his cheek against her forehead.

"Well, I don't think Pauline has bronchitis at all," he said.

Diver and Charlotte both looked dumbfounded.

"We had a major outbreak of the disease while I was in medical college in Philadelphia. Every doctor in town requested med students to act as assistants until the epidemic ceased. You might say, I've seen my share of the malady."

He picked up a towel Charlotte had hung on a

chair back and placed it over his shoulder. Cradling Pauline, he patted her back until she coughed up another spat of mucus: brown tinged.

"The first phase of treating the illness is determining whether the patient truly has bronchitis to start with. If not, which of the numerous other breathing issues could it be? It's amazing what an observant person can learn from a cough, a wheeze, a ragged breath, or the color of phlegm.

"This child's persistent cough, brown tinged mucus, high fever with chills, increased heart rate, and the crackling sound in her lungs?"

He looked at Pauline and blotted a dribble of spew from her cheek with the towel.

"If I were to venture a guess, I'd say she's a victim of pneumonia."

"Pneumonia!" gasped Diver. "Isn't that more dangerous than Bronchitis?"

"It can be," said Dulaney, "if not caught in time. Luckily, because of you being more alert to serious symptoms after what you endured with your son; you may have bought us the time we need. Many folks hold off thinking it's just a cold 'til it's too late. You didn't. I think we caught it early. If anyone has a chance of beating this thing, this child has." He handed Pauline back to Charlotte and began rolling up his sleeves. "And the thing about pneumonia is; once you beat it, it's gone."

That entire evening was spent caring for Pauline. Many of Dulaney's procedures were already familiar to Diver because of his extensive reading on Dennis' illness. They raised the head of Pauline's bassinet to help keep her airways clear. They boiled peppermint and honey in water to create a humidifying mist. They alternated feeding Pauline warm teas made of fresh peppermint, ginger and mullein to break-up the mucus. Dulaney even made a mullein poultice for Pauline's chest.

By midnight, with the child's breathing at a more even rate, and the phlegm seemingly under control, she finally dosed off.

"That's what she needs more than anything," said Dulaney. "Plenty of rest to let her body heal."

Charlotte stood holding Diver's arm as she rested her head on his shoulder. They were each consumed in their own thoughts as they watched their little girl sleep.

"Now, what we need to do is try and find out where the malady came from," said Dulaney.

"Where it came from?" questioned Charlotte.

"Yes," Dulaney said. "Pneumonia is contagious. If we can isolate the carrier, we may be able to prevent it from spreading."

Diver and Charlotte both shook their heads. They had no clue where it may have come from.

"Has anyone who seemed ill been near Pauline in the last few days?" asked Dulaney.

"No. No one's been here except Billy," said Charlotte, "and he seemed fine other than still nursing his injuries."

"How about mill customers?" he asked Diver.

"Ain't had any in the last week or so," said Diver. "Seasons over."

Charlotte got a puzzled look on her face. "You know, I did talk to Dolores at the B&C the other day," she said. "She was a bit choked up, but said it was from road dust. I remember she commented on Pauline's new blanket. But Pauline wasn't with me."

"Dolores Kilpatrick?" asked Dulaney.

Charlotte nodded.

Dolores! thought Dulaney. He knew she had been caring for Ollie's grandmother until her condition worsened to the point that they called him in. She hadn't shown any symptoms of illness while he was there, but it's not uncommon for pneumonia to develop over several days.

Problem with old folks is, they develop so many ailments that minic each other, it's hard to tell one complaint from the next. Death is usually attributed to 'old age'.

Yep, thought Dulaney, Dolores is the likely suspect.

Charlotte watched the gears turning in the doc's eyes. An unsettling fear clutched her heart.

"You don't think I brought this on to my own child, do you?" she asked.

"No, no!" said Dulaney. "I'm just looking for answers. We don't know it was Dolores, and even if it was, you couldn't have known."

"Oh, my sweet baby," Charlotte lamented. "What have I done?"

Diver wrapped her in his arms. "You've done

nothing, dear," he said, trying to allay her fears. "God knows how much you love that child."

"Amen," said Dulaney. But all the same, first thing tomorrow mornin' he was gonna do a wellness check on Dolores Kilpatrick.

Three hours after leaving the blue-tailed-lizard's abode; Mary figured he was probably more than happy to see them go, they stood in a small barren clearing atop a craggy mountain knoll. Wide eyed and speechless, they watched a column of gray-white smoke drift over a distant valley.

Having been raised in a community where fire was essential to their daily lives, they knew the difference between a cooking/heating fire and a wildfire.

This fire was confined — isolated. At worst a campfire, preferably a cabin fireplace.

Breaking her stupor, Mary turned to Susan. "Smoke like that can only mean one thing," she said.

The girls looked at each other. Their dirt smudged faces alight with excitement.

"People!" blurted Susan. "People! We're saved!"

They hugged, and cried, and jumped around like excited toddlers on their birthdays. For the first time since escaping the coyote cabin, they truly believed they were gonna make it home safe. All they had to do was cross a couple hidden hollows and top a few mid-sized ridges. Piece o' cake!

Epilogue

"Sorry to leave ya danglin' like that, but I done run off at the mouth till it's nigh on to milkin' time. I'd be plumb tickled to sit out here and jaw with y'all some more, but the missus and Betty Lou wouldn't take to kindly to it.

"See her down there now, utter full and chompin' at the nubbins bucket.

"That's Betty Lou, ya understand, not the missus.

"Anyway, y'all be sure to come on back and we'll see what ever become of them gals — Mary and Susan. Then there's me and Pauline and Pa and the whole gang.

"Yep, I reckon there's still a heap o' tellin' to do yet.

"Till next time, hug yer family, say howdy to yer neighbor, and God Bless.